HOW FIEVEL STOLE THE MOON

THE MOON

A Tale for Sweet Children and Sour Scholars

Richard P. Kluft

(Rishon Fischel ben Yaakov Moshe)

ISBN-13: 9780692249949
ISBN-10: 069224994X
Library of Congress Control Number: 2014945467
And the Horse You Rode in On Press, Bala Cynwyd PA

A Dedication for Sweet Children

For

Sofia, Daniel, and Safia

Stay As Wonderful As You Are

David, Jacqueline, & Dima

(Yeah, You're Still Sweet After All These Years!)

For My Dedication to Grown-up Professionals and
Sour Scholars,

Kindly Turn to the End of the Book, and Listen to Izzy.

A BRIEF NOTE ABOUT THE NAME
OF GOD (G-D)

Susan Levey, who is Temple Educator at Beth David Reform Congregation in Gladwyne, Pennsylvania, wisely encouraged me to include a brief prefatory note about the way the Jews in *How Fievel Stole the Moon...* speak of the Almighty.

God, hereafter to be written as "G-d," was always on the mind the observant Jews who are the central protagonists and antagonists of this book. My brief comments below barely touch upon the complexity of this important subject. They are so abbreviated that I fear they might offend a traditional Jewish reader.

The name of G-d most commonly found in the Torah is a four-letter word often referred to as the Tetragrammaton. YHWH is one of its many English transliterations. However, by the time of the Second Temple, centuries before the Common Era, speaking the name of G-d aloud had become restricted to certain prayers on holidays of profound importance. "Adonai" generally came to be spoken aloud in its place, but often the use of "Adonai" was restricted to occasions of prayer.

Over time observant Jews often came to use HaShem, which is Hebrew for "the Name," in most contexts, and to modify the written expression of G-d's name. For example, I do so when I omit the vowel "o" from the word "God." Other ways of expressing the name of G-d involve substituting for the word G-d one or more of G-d's attributes, as I did above, by using the term "Almighty".

Modern liberal Jews often are unfamiliar with these concerns, which remain matters of great important in more traditional branches of Judaism.

ONCE UPON A TIME IN GLADWYNE, LOWER MERION, PENNSYLVANIA

Folklore and folk stories have a number of fascinating characteristics. They are collective creations. They reflect the contributions of generations of authors over many, many years. They tend to grow and change over time. Ergo, they have unknown origins, a multitude of generally anonymous authors, and they often come to exist in several versions, often with strikingly different details, subplots, and outcomes.

In a charming way, they share certain features with urban legends and jazz. The stories in urban legends begin as creations, not as established facts. They take on lives of their own, often with unsettling momentum. Every teller of the tale within the legend is perforce both an innovator and the custodian of an established tradition, a tradition that is always in the process of becoming. So, when folk stories are written down or refined into literature, they are not so much being told as retold. Likewise, we may know the melodies and harmonies from which jazz musicians begin, but what they create from those beginnings is forever new, and may prove wonderfully different, astonishingly different, at times even unrecognizably different, set after vigorous set, session after session, year after year.

On a frigid Sunday in March, 2014 I took a break from working on a response to a very nasty and inaccurate attack on my scholarly work and professional reputation. My wife Estelle and I attended a Sunday morning talk at Beth David Reform Congregation in Gladwyne, Pennsylvania by Joseph Davis, Ph.D. Dr. Davis is a professor at Gratz College. His special area of interest is the study of 16th and 17th century Ashkenazi Jewish folklore. The comments on folklore and folk studies I made above were drawn directly from the notes I took at Professor Davis' lecture.

Professor Davis introduced us to the rich comedic and satiric traditions surrounding the Khakhomim of Chelm, the "wise men" of a legendary village of fools. Rightly or wrongly, the Chelm stories seemed to me to be the foundation of all I had come to understand as "Jewish Humor." Further, for reasons I cannot articulate, much of what I heard reminded me of aspects of the classical Greek comedies of Aristophanes, the satiric imaginary worlds of Jonathan Swift's masterpiece, *Gulliver's Travels*, and the early novels of contemporary satirist Carl Hiaasen.

Later that day, I found myself exhausted by my efforts to complete my scholarly response. I was distracted from my task both by my inability to understand how the collective "wisdom" of a distinguished collection of "wise men" had agreed to the publication of the article to which I now was laboring to respond, and by my intensifying curiosity about the world of Jewish folk stories and folklore, subjects about which I knew very little.

Forcing myself forward to write a defense of my work and my self that never should have been necessary, I grew progressively more bored and weary. Although I never take naps, on that one particular day, I fell asleep at my computer in the middle of the afternoon.

2

When I awakened from that very uncharacteristic nap, I was still in the grips of a very uncharacteristic dream indeed, a long and puzzling dream that must have been connected in some way to my attending Professor Davis' lecture, and to my frustrated wish to spend the afternoon surfing the net to learn more about Jewish folkloric traditions rather than flail away at crafting a scholarly rebuttal few if any would read or remember.

In my dream, at first I saw a Jewish shtetl of nearly 400 years ago, depicted in fascinating if fanciful detail. A pleasant-looking older man stood outside of a synagogue. He began to greet me. But before I had a chance to meet this man and immerse myself in imagining the lives of those who lived there, I found myself being drawn away, very much against my will.

Something was forcing me to take leave of that picturesque shtetl, some miles outside of Slonim, in a region that now is part of Poland, and compelling me instead to go heaven knows where to follow and bear witness to the misfortunes of Fievel ben Schmendrick, a hapless itinerant umbrella repairman. Fievel's real name was Fievel ben Yaakov Moshe, but a Schmendrick he was, as his father had been a Schmendrick before him. So, at least behind his back, Fievel ben Schmendrick he was called!

ONCE UPON A SCHMENDRICK

F ievel ben Yaakov Moshe, better known as Fievel ben Schmendrick (Fievel, the son of that Stupid Man), was a lonely and unhappy soul indeed.

Poor Fievel! Like his father before him, Fievel had grown up in a city in which Jews were treated kindly, and mingled easily with their gentile neighbors. Like his father before him, Fievel learned to manufacture and repair umbrellas for the rich and powerful gentile elite. This was not too many years before the invention of new fabrics allowed umbrellas to be made that would actually shield a person from the rain.

Today, we would call the objects of Fievel's craft and trade parasols, lovely creations made to shield the worthy and the wealthy from the sun, but useless in foul weather. In many places the privilege of carrying a parasol was restricted by law, because such an accouterment was considered a sign of patrician breeding, wealth, nobility, power, and high station in life.

No Jew could carry a parasol, but Jews were allowed make and to repair them. Fievel Ben Yaakov Moshe had mastered this trade just in time for the Duke of the province in which his family resided, a benevolent nobleman who was quite tolerant of his Jewish and Moslem subjects, even fond of them and pleased with the skills and commerce that they brought to his domain, to die of a fever and be succeeded by his eldest son. The kind Duke's eldest son generously allowed the Jews and Moslems in his realm a full week to leave, to convert, or to be impaled on a stake in the courtyard of his castle.

Fievel's softhearted father, reluctant to abandon his aged and arthritic ox, patiently endured the beast's slow progress en route toward parts unknown. His family crossed beyond the duchy's border only moments before pursuing priests and soldiers, obedient to the new duke's cruel orders to convert or kill any Jews and Moslems who remained within his domain, would have fallen upon them, determined to destroy their faith, their very lives, or both.

Fievel's softheaded father was reluctant to disappoint his wife, long homesick for the place or her birth, or to abandon his trade, even though it could be practiced profitably only among the gentile elite. Eventually he brought his family to the tiny shtetl where his wife's family still lived, but where no affluent gentiles resided. Soon he was reduced to abject poverty, and passed away.

After a year of mourning, his father's bereaved wife married a widowed furrier, and over the next few months Fievel, the son of Yaakov Moshe, who had many of his hapless father's shortcomings and failings, slowly came to realize that his presence in their household was unwelcome. He no longer had a home.

Sadly, Fievel packed his few belongings in a small sack. He left that tiny shtetl and the home of his mother and her new family behind him, and began to live a wandering life. Walking from castle to castle, he offered his services to repair the fine parasols of the local nobility wherever he roamed. Fievel was an honest, kindly man who never ceased to be confused and bewildered by what had befallen him.

All his life, Fievel had heard tales of Chelm, that celebrated city in which communities of Jews and gentiles lived side by side in peace and harmony. Surely there he would find a place, however humble, among his fellow Jews! Surely there he would find enough affluent gentiles to make use of his very special skills and services!

So, in the fullness of time, Fievel ben Yaakov Moshe, Fievel ben Schmendrick, began his journey to the wonderful city of Chelm. In Fievel's mind, Chelm was indeed a place of legend! Prosperous gentiles living in harmony with a Jewish community renowned as a seat of learning and scholarship! What could be better?

The wise men of its Jewish community, the legendary Khakhomim of Chelm, were famous for their great scholarship, their unique interpretations of the Torah and the Talmud, and the rapidity with which they resolved deep and twisted problems of profound ethical, legal, and scholarly complexity. As he set off for Chelm, his heart was light.

WHAT SCHMUEL'S UNCLE TOLD SCHMUEL, AND WHAT SCHMUEL TOLD FIEVEL LONG, LONG AGO

And yet... And yet years ago, back in the city of his childhood, back in the days of the kind old duke, his friend, Schmuel ben David, had traveled to Chelm with his uncle when Schmuel was still a boy. On his return, he had told Fievel many stories about Chelm, and he even had warned Fievel that some people, his uncle among them, were not so sure about these famous Khakhomim.

"My uncle saw this with his own eyes! He heard this with his own ears! He was sent to deliver a fine horse, bred hereabouts by Mendel ben Ezekiel, to the Chief Rabbi of Chelm. You know, Fievel, in our grandparents' time our people were not allowed to own or ride horses. Perhaps times are improving for the Jews! Who knows?

"So, when we arrived, I was sleepy. So he left me behind at an inn, and went to bring the horse to the great man. But he learned that the Chief Rabbi, may Adonai bless his name, had convened their Sanhedrin. Twenty-three learned members of the Chief Rabbi's congregation were sitting in session, holding court for the Jewish community of Chelm. They had assembled in the largest room in the beit midrash at the synagogue, a place of study and deep thought, its shelves overflowing with holy books and learned texts.

"They were about to conclude their business for the day with a final prayer, and rest or take a nosh before evening services…. Who knows? …. When a man of their community, well known to them all, burst into their meeting place in a state of high emotion.

"'Great Rabbi and Wise Men of Chelm! I come to you for justice! My situation is urgent! I must be heard at once!'

"Before my uncle could say, 'Honored Rabbi, before you solve this problem, please…. Where should I bring your new horse?', twenty-four beards turned as one in the direction of this new supplicant.

"They did everything just right, Fievel! First they said a prayer to welcome the supplicant, Yashua ben Levi. Then they said a prayer to HaShem, imploring him to grant them wisdom in their deliberations. And finally, the Chief Rabbi offered up a special prayer, asking HaShem to purge a nasty smell that had suddenly filled the room.

"Only then, the Chief Rabbi turned toward Yashua ben Levi. 'As unworthy as we are,' he said, 'we will apply our knowledge of the wisdom and traditions of our people to offer you the help you seek. Tell us what is troubling you.'

"'Distinguished Rabbi! Noble Khakhomim!' Yashua began. 'What an indignity! I purchased such a nice fish from Mordecai ben Tsuris down by the river! He wrapped it in straw and cloth. Since I was already carrying other things, I tucked it into my shirt for safekeeping. Just as I was talking to the lovely widow Rifka, suddenly the tail of this awful creature popped out and swiped me in the face. I was humiliated! Completely humiliated! How can I continue to court this pious and proper woman of good character after suffering such awful shame before her? Good Khakhomim, she laughed so hard that she fainted, right there on the street! Such a shanda! I demand justice against this fish, the very evil beast that just destroyed my honor, my manhood, and my future happiness!'

"He began to open his shirt to display the culprit, but no sooner had the first two buttons been unbuttoned than the Chief Rabbi proclaimed the problem of the nasty smell understood, blessed be Adonai, and asked Yashua to refasten those two buttons once again, as quickly as he could.

"But then the Chief Rabbi paused, thought, and reconsidered. 'But under the rules of our proceedings,' he said, 'we must examine the accused! No matter how offensive the stench, we must endure it. It is written that the accused must be allowed to face his accuser!'

"Some younger men not yet holy or accomplished enough to sit on the Sanhedrin were summoned. Soon the accused lay on a thick mat of straw before the eyes of those who would judge its fate. Indeed, it was a magnificent beast, large and fat! But wait!

"One of the older members of the Sanhedrin cried out, as if he could not believe what he saw, 'This fish has no scales! It is not kosher!' Indeed, on further inspection, the prominent whiskers at its snout, not unlike those of the youngest of the men assisting the Sanhedrin, declared the offending beast to be a catfish, unfit for consumption by a Jew!

"'How could Mordecai ben Tsuris have sold such a fish to me?' cried Yashua, the plaintiff. 'I never suspected I would be betrayed by a fellow Jew! He could not have done this. No! I don't remember this fish. This is not the fish I bought.'

"The Chief Rabbi immediately summoned Mordecai the fish-seller to appear before the Sanhedrin. When he arrived, Yashua immediately gave him a meaningful glance. Then, Yashua told his tale once again. First, he recounted his purchase of the fish from Mordecai, and then he described the creature's astonishingly impertinent behavior. Mordecai looked hard at Yashua, shrugged, and nodded. An expression of shock and complete bewilderment swept over his face as he turned to face the Chief Rabbi.

"'Honored Rabbi! Gentlemen and scholars of the Sanhedrin! Indeed, Yashua speaks the truth! How could I, a righteous Jew, have sold Yashua, an even more devoted and righteous Jewish man than I, a fish that was not kosher? Unthinkable!'

"On the mat, the unholy fish continued to gasp, its mouth opening and closing as if gulping in the air, its gill flaps flaring out widely as well.

"The Khakhomim of Chelm circled the fish, staring hard. Finally, one cried, 'It is looking at me! What evil will this demon fish wreak upon us?'

"The Chief Rabbi turned to Mordecai. 'Is that fish still breathing?' he asked.

"'Yes, learned Rabbi!'

"'Very well,' said the Rabbi. He closed his eyes and turned away from the others, moving his lips in silence and seeming to be lost in prayer. After several minutes he opened his eyes and turned back to address the others.

"'It is clear to me that this fish is an evil creature capable to changing its form and appearance. It has changed from a kosher fish with scales that breathes the water, the fish sold by Mordecai to Yashua, into this unholy creature without scales that breathes the air. Quick! Let us throw it back in the water before it can change its shape again. We shall drown it!'

"'Now, me, Schmuel,' my uncle said, 'Me, I would have thought that either Mordecai had duped that other fool, or that the two struck up a deal so Mordecai could sell a fish he otherwise could not sell. I would have thought that other stupid man was so overcome by his shame before Rifka that in the moment he thought only of revenge for his humiliation and forgot that he had violated the laws of HaShem. The fish he had bought for dinner, that now lay accused before the Sanhedrin, was not kosher. And now, if he did not lie, he himself might face the wrath of the Sanhedrin! But maybe I was wrong.'

"They placed the big fish on a cart, and everyone accompanied the Chief Rabbi and the Khakhomim down to a little river nearby, a branch of what we here call the Bug. Just before they threw the fish to its death, the youngest and least prestigious member of the Sanhedrin spoke up, with many profound apologies and great hesitation. He asked Yashua and Mordecai to step away from the members of the Sanhedrin for a moment while he shared his concerns.

"'Great Rabbi! Learned members of the Sanhedrin! What if these men are not telling us the truth? What if this is just a plain catfish, although a big one, and what if Mordecai the fish-seller offered this trafe fish to Yashua at a bargain price because it was not kosher. Should we not consider that perhaps it was both sold by a man and purchased by a man both more respectful of their pocket-books than of the laws of Kashrut?'

"The Great Rabbi's face grew grim. He gestured for Mordecai and Yashua to come back to where the Sanhedrin stood.

"'Throw that demon fish to its watery grave, and stand by with poles to prevent it from coming on shore again and breathing air!

"'And throw this miserable wretch who dishonors these two men and the Khakhomim of Chelm, throw this man into the waves with the demon fish he respects more than his fellow Jews! And if this blasphemer emerges from the waters alive, he shall have no place among us. The doors of our synagogue are closed to him and his family.'

"The twenty-three remaining beards wagged their learned agreements."

"And what happened?" asked Fievel.

"The fish swam away. The man did not seem to know how to swim. I do not know his fate. The rabbi wondered whether he, too, was a demon. Perhaps he now had assumed the form of a fish in order to escape? No matter – Once he went under the water, my uncle said, he was seen no more.

"So, either those two men lied, or that beast changed back into a normal fish faster than the rabbi had thought possible. Here, near

Slonim, I will tell you that the two men lied. There, in Chelm, I would tell you, and you must believe this if you travel to Chelm, that it is a fact that a strange and evil fish threatened the good Jews of Chelm, and only the intervention of the Great Rabbi and the Sanhedrin of Chelm saved their community from disaster."

This all made Fievel's thoughts whirl around in his head like the dry leaves of autumn in the cold winds of December. He lay sleepless that night so many distant years ago, wondering about the man who was thrown into the river for disagreeing with the Great Rabbi and the Sanhedrin. But when Schmuel had told him this story, Fievel was but a boy, a boy who probably had thought that after all, it was just a silly story, and never imagined he would someday travel to the distant city of Chelm.

FIEVEL'S ARRIVAL AND HARD TIMES IN THE CITY OF CHELM

In the fullness of time, Fievel, still determined but now nearly penniless, made his way to Chelm. While indeed there were many aristocratic and affluent gentiles in Chelm, very few considered parasols fashionable. Finding barely enough work to put a crust of bread in his mouth, Fievel lodged in a shed in the yard of the home of a pious widow, whose husband had drowned several years before. Every night his stomach growled with hunger. The widow was kind, but had little enough for herself, and nothing to share.

"It is difficult to be a widow in a hard world," Fievel remarked on one cold night before he repaired to his shed. They spoke at her door, because he could not pass through her door and be alone with a proper woman under the roof of her home.

"If it is not unkind of me to ask," said Fievel, "what misfortune befell your husband and left you alone?"

"You are a kind man, Fievel. To this very day, I wonder. When I cry myself to sleep night after night, I wonder and wonder. My late husband, of blessed memory, was the newest member of the Sanhedrin. He felt so honored to be selected. One terrible day the Sanhedrin had just finished its deliberations when Yashua ben Levi rushed in to complain that a fish possessed by a dybbuk or some evil thing had attacked him. The Sanhedrin examined the accused fish. It changed shape right in front of them! The Chief Rabbi determined that the fish was indeed possessed by a demon, and that at that moment it needed to breathe air. He ordered the beast to be thrown into the river and drowned. Alas, as that terrible demon disguised as a fish was thrown into the water, in mid-air it became a fish that could breathe in the water! It seized my husband, carrying him down to a watery grave. Only the wisdom of the Great Rabbi prevented the death of the entire Sanhedrin!"

This must be the man Schmuel's uncle had seen thrown... But just as Fievel began to formulate how to tell the widow what Schmuel's uncle had seen and heard, Schmuel's uncle's words of warning rose to stop his tongue. "Here, near Slonim, I will tell you that the two men lied. There, in Chelm, I would tell you, and you must believe this if you travel to Chelm, that it is a fact that a strange and evil fish threatened the good Jews of Chelm, and only the intervention of the Great Rabbi and the Sanhedrin of Chelm saved their community from disaster."

Fievel tried to be wise, though it filled his heart with pain to do so.

"What a wonder it is that such a remarkable man serves the Jews of Chelm with such righteousness and courage! I will be sure to attend synagogue tomorrow and every day while I am in Chelm!" He tried not to choke as he struggled to speak these words.

FIEVEL COMES UNDER SCRUTINY AND SUSPICION

So it was that Fievel, who had little else with which to occupy his time, began to attend the synagogue of the Great Rabbi of Chelm. At first, he attracted little notice. After all, Jewish peddlers came along from time to time, bearing cloth, needles, spices, and all manner of goods. Students bound from one yeshiva to another, scholars eager to visit all the great thinkers – every few weeks one or more strangers might be welcomed into the congregation.

But after a week or so, there was Fievel -- still. Some of the men spoke to him. Did he have news of the greater world? Was he a sage? Was he a match for a daughter who somehow, unkindly, had been overlooked by the men of that place?

No. Fievel was not any one of those things. He was just an observant Jew down on his luck, reduced to living in a little shack. That is, until Rebecca, the oldest spinster among the Jewish women of Chelm, sent her nephew to follow him home. Who knows why? There is no one left to say. Some people just love to stir up trouble for reasons of their own. Only the wisdom of HaShem understands such things!

The boy watched Fievel open the gate to the widow's yard and walk to the little shed where he resided. He returned to his aunt, and told her what he saw. Within minutes, the spinster Rebecca sent the boy running to tell his tale to the Great Rabbi.

"'A shanda!' says my Aunt Rebecca! 'A single man living with the widow woman! An offense to the Almighty!'"

"Convene the Sanhedrin!" the Great Rabbi ordered, and then fussed in confusion until he found the right prayer to say. "A shanda!"

THE FERVENT FIND FAULT
WITH FIEVEL

A great room full of beards and blessings heard the boy's report. This time, matters were not so clear. Everyone knew the widow was very poor. Everyone knew that the itinerant parasol repairman made very little money. Everyone knew that both were pious Jews, and that there were no terrible and immoral acts to condemn.

But yet! If the widow's house was her house, and Fievel lived elsewhere than her house, then the poor pittance Fievel paid in rent might be a mitzvah, a good deed that kept the widow from hunger. Indeed, once pleasingly plump, the widow had become quite slender in recent years. Little kindness had come her way. But! If the shed was indeed part of the widow's house, then Fievel lived in the widow's house, and this could not be!

There was much sympathy within the Sanhedrin for both the widow and for Fievel. At first it seemed that everything just might be resolved with kindness and compassion.

"But yet!" observed the Chief Rabbi, "On Shabbat and the Holy Days, when we are not allowed to travel, we extend a string from our house of prayer to the furthest homes of our community, to tell the Lord that everyone is already in our synagogue, so it is not a sin to walk from one place in the synagogue to another!"

He led a procession of twenty-some of the Khakhomim of Chelm, a full Sanhedrin, down to the home of the widow. There, a pathetic, dilapidated fence with a nearly shattered gate surrounded her tiny property, house, yard, and shed. The tattered fence touched both the back of the shed and one side of the widow's house.

"No! This cannot be!" cried the Great Rabbi. "They are living in the same house! They are living in sin! Our laws forbid such shameful deeds!"

He summoned the terrified widow to her door. "Shame upon you! You are living in sin! You must marry this man today or be banished forever from our congregation! You will have no place among the righteous women of Chelm!"

In vain, the weeping woman wailed that she would remain true to her late husband until the day she died!

"Very well!" The Chief Rabbi summoned some men who were young and strong, but who were not deemed fit or prepared to become members of the Sanhedrin. He ordered them to tear down the shed where Fievel lived, barely sheltered from the wind and rain.

When Fievel returned after yet another day of failing to find work, he found his squalid little home was now no more than a pile of splinters, and all his tools were tossed about or broken. He was banished, turned away from the synagogue door.

That night, as the widow wept, Fievel, evicted from his hovel and his people by the Great Rabbi's edict, faced the dark and dreary night alone and without shelter. Poor Fievel! He prayed he would survive that terrible night. He had no place to rest his weary head. So he walked, and then he stumbled, and then he staggered for hours through the darkest alleys of Chelm.

After the Great Rabbi had spoken, all doors, even the doors of humblest sheds and barns, were barred to him. Even nearby gentile homeowners turned away as he passed. As he walked all night through the town of Chelm, he leaned furtively, whenever he could, against the warm walls near the fireplaces of the snug warm homes he was forbidden to enter, begging Adonai to preserve him from the chill.

So things went for Fievel and the widow, day after dreary day, and night after bone-chilling night. Every now and then a kind Jew or Gentile would pretend to drop a crust of bread, or some other bit of food, look at it in feigned disgust, and walk away. Fievel grew lean, and then he became gaunt, but somehow, he survived. He could not afford to stay. He could not afford to go.

ON A FINE SPRING DAY, A RABBI FROM BERDICHEVA, A MAN OF KINDNESS, SET OUT FOR VILNA

As it so happened, with the arrival of spring, the Rabbi of Berdicheva, a kind and gentle scholar, had reason to pass through Chelm on his journey to Vilna. In Vilna he would revisit the places of his childhood, and perhaps see some of his family for the last time. The rabbi was a lively, spirited man, but far too wise to imagine that he would remain so forever. Already in his seventies, he knew that this tender spring offered him a chance to see for one last time the people and places he loved, but had left behind to lead a congregation so very far away. Three promising students traveled with him.

His coming through Chelm was great news, carried ahead by other travelers who had learned of his plans and spoken of them to others as they went along their ways. Although the rabbi from Berdicheva did not wish to tarry, he felt he could not decline the pleas of the

Great Rabbi of Chelm, carried to him in messages born by travelers who were journeying back toward Berdicheva. The Great Rabbi of Chelm begged the rabbi from Berdicheva to honor the Jewish community of Chelm by addressing his congregation, and by studying Torah and discussing the Talmud with the famed Khakhomim of Chelm. Though his heart pulled him toward Vilna with more and more urgency, the Rabbi of Berdicheva was a man who found it difficult to deny the requests of his fellow scholars, his fellow Jews.

THE INNKEEPER'S TALE -- OF
CATFISH AND CHELM

As they drew nearer to Chelm, the rabbi from Berdicheva saw that he and the three students who accompanied him would not reach the city itself before darkness fell. They took lodging at an inn near Keszlow, where they could rest and restore themselves before the last several miles of their journey.

As they dined, the innkeeper, a congenial man, conversed with them and learned they were going to travel through Chelm.

"Ah! Chelm! A holy but confusing place! A place of great scholarship and wisdom beyond my understanding."

"Surely not, my good host," said the rabbi, "You seem like a very intelligent fellow."

"To tell you the truth, Rabbi, I do become confused by the wisdom of the Khakhomim of Chelm. Here in Keszlow men see me as a man of good character and understanding. But when I go to Chelm.... When I go to Chelm.... I suddenly find I understand nothing, nothing at all. The Khakhomim of Chelm are men of genius, I know, but sometimes their wisdom is so profound that I can hardly grasp a thing they say. Their deep thoughts make my head whirl."

"Can you give us an example?" asked young Yossi, a still impetuous but promising young scholar.

"Surely this good man has important things to do, Yossi. We should not keep him from his tasks," said the rabbi from Berdicheva. "Be still, Yossi. You too, Judah and Yaakov!"

"Well, honored master and young gentlemen, it would relieve me to share my sense of confusion."

When the rabbi nodded assent, the innkeeper sat with them. The innkeeper told the rabbi and his students of the miseries of Fievel, huddling against warm walls in the cold dark nights, and of the anguish of the widow, growing leaner and leaner, and of the amazing and profoundly disturbing story of the dybbuk fish.

The Rabbi of Berdicheva saw the eyes of his students rolling in disbelief. While tempted to join them, he struggled to maintain decorum.

"Perhaps, my good man, when I arrive at Chelm, I may find myself as confused as you, if not more so. These tales surpass my understanding."

The innkeeper indeed was a man of great insight. "Thank you, Rabbi. You have no idea how much better I feel. Thank you." He placed a bottle of his best wine before the rabbi and his party, and bid them good night.

"Rabbi! Rabbi! What is he saying?" asked Judah. "Can a dybbuk inhabit a fish?" "Can a fish pull a man into the water?" asked Yaakov. And "Can a rabbi find in the good books any reason to starve two good people, breaking all of our rules of charity and kindness?" wondered Yossi.

"We will have much to learn in Chelm," said the rabbi. Noticing Yossi's smirk, he pretended great indignation. "Yossi! A rabbi must be respectful – of his G-d, of his fellow Jews, of all men...."

"And of large catfish?" asked Yossi. The innkeeper, realizing that he had forgotten to clear the last of the dinner dishes, had returned to the room at that very moment to collect them.

"No! No! No! Never say 'catfish' in Chelm! There is a legend that if you say 'catfish' in Chelm, a demon will take your life!" He rushed from the room.

The rabbi thought, and then shook his head.

"To prayer and to bed with all of you! Now! I have much to contemplate."

Alone, with good wine and blessed silence, the rabbi from Berdicheva carefully pondered what he had heard.

"Could the legends handed down from years long ago be true?" he wondered. "No! They could not be true! But yet, how can I deny the meaning of the evidence that has been put before me?"

THE MISSION OF A MIGHTY ANGEL, A TALE OF TWO SACKS, AND THE DESPAIR OF ADONAI

The rabbi from Berdicheva, like all learned Jewish men of his day, had heard and discussed an old tale, long told among Talmudic scholars, that recounts the journey of a mighty angel whom G-d had sent to earth on a mission of the greatest importance. The angel brought two large sacks to the people Israel. The first sack was full of wisdom, a gift from HaShem to be distributed among the congregations of the world. The second was empty. The angel was instructed to fill that sack with all the foolishness he could collect, and thereby to remove the burden of all that foolishness from the Jewish people and from their fellow men.

This task demanded every ounce of the angel's strength. Yes, with every bit of wisdom the angel bestowed, the sack of wisdom grew lighter and lighter. But, the sack of foolishness! It became heavier and heavier more quickly than the sack of wisdom grew lighter and lighter. The angel had been chosen for this mission because he was the strongest angel among all the hosts of heaven, but toward the end of his exertions, even he had nearly succumbed to exhaustion and fatigue.

Finally, at last, the mighty angel completed his task. Wisdom had been delivered to all the Jewish communities of the world. He caught his heavenly breath, and began to make his ascent toward the throne of G-d. But as he soared toward heaven, that second sack, already about to burst at its seams from its terrible burden, the weight of every bit of the world's human foolishness, began to come apart. It tore open just as he climbed skyward over the Jewish community of Chelm.

Upon his return to heaven the mortified angel suddenly realized that the second sack must have given way, and that all of its contents had fallen back into the world. Faster than the flight of an eagle, he soared back to earth. But too late! Alas, too late!

When the sack had given way, the Jews of Chelm, in an instant, had been transformed into a city of fools! When the angel returned to earth, and learned where the collected foolishness of the world had fallen, he discovered that the citizens of Chelm had embraced their sudden and unexpected gift as if it had bestowed a very special divine wisdom upon them. They could not be persuaded to part with it!

Adonai's response is commemorated in the lore of heaven as the first occasion on which a new word would be created and used, a new word that would make its way into the languages of many peoples throughout the world, a word that would spread even more widely than the fame of the wise Khakhomim of Chelm –

"Oy!" exclaimed Adonai. "Oy! Oy! Oy!"

And the angels echoed, "Oy! Oy! Oy! -- Oy! Oy! Oy!"

Before he drifted off to sleep, the rabbi from Berdicheva lingered over a prayer he had never before uttered to HaShem, "Oh Blessed One! Let that legend be no more than a legend, just a fantastic story to amuse children. Please let me find men of true wisdom and kindness in the city of Chelm!"

As he snuffed out his candle, was that a laugh that the rabbi from Berdicheva seemed to hear in the darkness? And then for a moment another sound... Was that the soft flutter of wings?

"Am I going insane to think that HaShem has heard my prayers, and sent an angel to warn me?" But before he could begin to wonder, the rabbi from Berdicheva drifted off, into a sweet dream of peace.

A MORNING AMONG GOOD MEN

As the next day began, the rabbi from Berdicheva and his students accompanied the innkeeper to the tiny synagogue of Keszlow for morning prayers. The local rabbi was overwhelmed by his distinguished visitor and invited him to lead the minyan of Keszlow in their worship. The rabbi from Berdicheva instead asked only to worship and study with the good men of Keszlow, and indeed found the Rabbi of Keszlow to be a man of deep thought. Many times he smiled and his eyes brightened as he relished the insights of this humble and uncelebrated sage. Once, he even exclaimed, "Aha. So that is what Adonai wants us to understand! My eyes had not been open to seeing that!"

The Rabbi of Berdicheva and his students, the modest Rabbi of Keszlow, and the simple farmers and small merchants of that place rejoiced in the Torah, the pilpul of the Talmud, and in one another, fellow seekers after the meaning of G-d's truth.

"But we have heard nothing to guide us from the great Rabbi of Berdicheva!" exclaimed one young farmer.

The rabbi from Berdicheva smiled, but said nothing. Just when the silence had begun to feel uncomfortable, Yossi dared to speak.

"May I gather from your silence, Rabbi, that you wish us to understand that all wisdom comes from G-d, and that you took delight in how G-d's wisdom found a voice in the thoughtful Rabbi of Keszlow?"

The rabbi from Berdicheva smiled, placed his hand on his young student's shoulder, and said, with tears of joy in his eyes, "Yes, and finally in the usually impetuous Yossi of Berdicheva!" And he laughed a laugh of such all-embracing love and celebration that it was taken up by the angels and thence carried up to the throne of G-d!

AN AFTERNOON AMONG THE
KHAKHOMIM OF CHELM

By the time the rabbi from Berdicheva and his students arrived at the synagogue in Chelm, it was early in the afternoon. There the Great Rabbi of Chelm was leading a learned discussion with his many students and admirers, all gathered together in a large room. A student heard the sounds of men arriving at the synagogue. He left his place among the scholars, and opened its door for the rabbi from Berdicheva and his party. He ushered them back to the big room in which the scholarly discussion was in progress. They entered through a door out of sight of the Great Rabbi of Chelm, who was seated in a comfortable chair facing away from that door while he spoke.

As the student turned away, to inform the Great Rabbi, the rabbi from Berdicheva gestured for him to stop, and not to interrupt the scholarly discourse already underway. He and his party sat quietly behind the Great Rabbi as his remarks drew to their conclusion.

"So, you see, when we are asked which is the most valuable in the eyes of G-d, the sun or the moon, we easily arrive at the answer," said the Great Rabbi. He paused dramatically before continuing, "Ah! It is the moon! Of course! And the reason? Ah! The reason is this – When it is dark, the moon gives us some light. But during the day, it is bright already! So, who really needs the sun? But we love the and value the sun anyway, just as we value every bit of HaShem's creation!"

As the many bearded heads nodded in unison, some with smiles of delight, the student who had opened the synagogue's door for the Rabbi of Berdicheva made the Great Rabbi of Chelm aware of his arrival.

In the privacy of his mind, the rabbi from Berdicheva was uttering a prayer, also a prayer he had never voiced before. "Dear Creator of the Universe, last night I prayed that I would find that the legend of the two sacks was no more than a folk tale. That was a selfish prayer. Today I implore you to help me understand..." But words failed the Rabbi of Berdicheva. Where should he start in begging for sufficient wisdom and guidance? But, perhaps the confused incompletion of his prayer spoke most clearly to Adonai.

Before the rabbi from Berdicheva and his students joined the Khakhomim of Chelm in their studies and deliberations, he took Yossi, Yaakov, and Judah aside and spoke to them briefly.

"I have prayed to Adonai for guidance. This is a strange place, and what kind of strange place it is, I leave to the G-d of our people, of all people to explain. If HaShem thinks it wise to do so, we will be enlightened. But among the Jews of Chelm, and among the gentiles of Chelm, we must be sure to find ways of expressing our interest and delight, and choose words with which we can avoid confrontations. It is always possible to say, 'I had not thought of the matter this way,' or, 'What a useful insight! I will have to ponder where it leads our thoughts,' or..."

But his instructions were cut short as the Great Rabbi of Chelm cried out, "Bring a comfortable chair like my own for our visitor! Come, our distinguished scholar and guest! Honor me by sitting by my side, and let us enjoy the sweetness of studying the wisdom that G-d has bestowed on his people Israel!"

So, the legends are true, thought the rabbi from Berdicheva as he took a seat of honor. Two sacks. Two sacks. And never speak of catfish!

OF THE NEED TO BE GREAT

Talmudic scholars may be compared with fighters. Unless, of course, they are listening! But the two rabbis began their discussions tentatively, avoiding any major skirmishes and gradually coming to appreciate each other's predilections, and each other's strengths and weaknesses. And each wondered how to demonstrate the rectitude or novel strengths of his insights without showing disrespect to thoughts of the other, without treading on the fringes of each other's prayer shawls, on the tzitzits of each other's talleisim.

The two rabbis managed to pass a completely congenial afternoon, although the rabbi from Berdicheva and his students suffered a certain degree of injury and discomfort due to the frequency with which they had to bite their tongues.

All went well until just before time for evening prayers. As they broke from their study, one of the disciples of the Great Rabbi of Chelm thought that perhaps their guests from Berdicheva might not fully appreciate the astonishing wisdom and power of their Great Rabbi of Chelm. After describing the sagacity with which the Great Rabbi had prevented the shanda of Fievel's living in the widow's shed, and the wisdom of severing these two shameful individuals from the shelter of the Jewish community, he began to tell the story of the terrible monster fish that had assaulted Yashua, the fish that had made Mordecai look like a goniff before the Jews of Chelm, the fish that had even destroyed a member of their own Sanhedrin. But the Great Rabbi of Chelm had brought that fearsome menace to an end, surely saving many, many lives.

"Such a creature! It began as a normal fish, plump and fat, the kind anyone would bring home for a dinner. And then, with no warning, it struck out at Yashua, a man who sits among us today," he said, pointing to Yashua ben Levi. "And by the time we confronted this fish before the Sanhedrin, it had transformed itself into a creature of the evil force. You should have seen…. No! No! Honored Rabbi, better that you did not see! A terrible beast, I tell you! And many of us saw it with our own eyes! And someone was foolish enough to think it was a catfish. Ptoey! We never say that word except to remember the deeds of our Great Rabbi that fateful day."

"What a day!" said the rabbi from Berdicheva, "Thanks be to G-d that you Khakhomim and your Great Rabbi were faced with this dilemma and found your way to the truth of it. Because, from all that you have said, I would not have been capable of such a task!

"To me, well… I would have been one of those fools who might have said, 'That sounds like a catfish. That is what they do. That is how they act.'"

"But honored rabbi, if you had seen its whiskers!"

"You mean little whiskers like young Yossi's?"

"Yes, honored Rabbi."

"I tell you, revered Khakhomim of Chelm, I would have been fooled. To me, it sounds like a catfish. A wels catfish. They grow big enough to swallow a child, maybe even a man. But Yashua is here, and an honorable man among you, and your Great Rabbi had the opportunity to study that creature. I did not.

"I tell you, revered Khakhomim of Chelm, to an old man from Berdicheva, it sounds like a catfish and perhaps some confusion about its appearance. But! You were there, and I was not.

"Evidence, my dear friends, evidence is so helpful in driving error from our minds! I am sure that my hastily formed reflections, which are really no more than an ignorant guess, bear no weight at all measured against your own experience and understanding. Only a fool would put a feather in the balance against an ingot of solid gold! A demon fish it must have been! I wonder if that demon fish… I suppose that it may have been able to change its size as well as its shape. That other man was never found? Do you suppose it might have swallowed that man?

"There are so many mysteries in the world that Adonai has created for us poor mortals! In a thousand lifetimes a man could never grasp and understand them all! Ah! It is time for prayer! It has been a most informative day, for which I thank you, Great Rabbi and Honored Khakhomim of Chelm."

THE UNFORTUNATE
CONTEMPLATIONS OF THE CHIEF
RABBI OF CHELM

Although the Chief Rabbi of Chelm could not quite understand, something upset him. Had he noticed a brief bemused twinkle in his visitor's eye just before he resumed the formal politeness that was his usual demeanor? As he returned to his quarters to prepare for evening prayers, he could not escape the worry that perhaps his distinguished visitor's true opinion of him might be other than the opinion expressed in his flattering words.

On the one hand, the Chief Rabbi of Chelm was delighted to be able to say that the learned Berdichever had confirmed his understanding of these arcane and challenging matters before the Sanhedrin of Chelm and his own entourage of disciples. On the other hand, the Chief Rabbi could not escape the feeling that something was amiss, that he still needed to do something more, something especially impressive, to demonstrate the full extent of his wisdom and his power, especially his righteousness and spiritual strength.

Accordingly, after the rabbi from Berdicheva and his students had left for their rooms in the home of the hospitable Mottel ben Zvi, a prosperous and burly butcher whose oldest children had married and moved into homes of their own, the Great Rabbi of Chelm remained restless and ill at ease. His mind found no peace, no comfort, no tranquility.

THE RABBI FROM BERDICHEVA, MOTTEL THE BUTCHER, AND THE TERROR WROUGHT BY CATFISH

As the evening passed into night, the rabbi from Berdicheva sent his students to bed. Then he sat in conversation for some time with Mottel, his host, a most congenial man.

"Mottel, I am a stranger here. I am struggling to understand as best I can. I hear about this astonishing creature from the river. I don't understand this beast, and I doubt that I ever will. But I do want to understand about these two people who have been cast out of the congregation and the community of Chelm."

Mottel looked around to be sure no one else was about.

"Rabbi, I often think that I myself am completely unable to understand the decisions of the Chief Rabbi and the learned Khakhomim of Chelm."

He looked about again, and then continued.

"Years ago, when that fish was brought before the Sanhedrin, I was a young man. Because I was young, strong, and unworthy to sit in the Sanhedrin, I was one of those who was summoned to carry that creature to where it was judged, to the cart in which it was placed, and to cast it into the waters to its death."

He looked around again.

"The great ones ponder the mind of G-d. I am not wise enough to fathom even the minds of my fellow man. You may have heard that a member of the Sanhedrin was taken to his death by that creature from hell. Rabbi, it looked like a plain old catfish to me. And maybe because I lacked the wisdom to see that it was not a catfish, but some awful beast or demon, I also was not wise enough to see how it dragged that man to his death."

"What do you recall? I am so confused that I would be grateful for anything you could tell me."

"Rabbi, I was young. I have never been a very intelligent man. But to my untutored ears and eyes, the youngest member of the Sanhedrin wondered aloud whether Mordecai the fish-seller had sold Yashua a trafe fish at a bargain price, and when the fish's tail slapped his face, in his shame he ran to the Sanhedrin, forgetting in his rage that if he purchased a catfish, it was a shanda." He fell silent.

"And?" the rabbi from Berdicheva pursued.

"And. And. And. And the Great Rabbi declared that if this unrighteous man favored the demon fish over the word of two pious members of his own congregation, he must be thrown into the river as well as the fish, and was never to return to the congregation of Chelm if he emerged from the river."

"And?"

"And. And. And. And the members of the Sanhedrin closest to him threw him into the river, and he was never seen again. It is his widow, childless and alone, who gave shelter to poor Fievel, permitting him to stay in a run-down shed in her yard. This unfortunate Fievel is a man who repairs parasols, and has found very little work. Both the luckless widow and this poor parasol mender are on the verge of starving.

"Rabbi, HaShem has been kind to my family. Until our rabbi's decree I would leave food at the widow's back door, and at the shed, and steal away unnoticed. But after his decree, often men watched her home, and I had to stop, may G-d forgive me." The burly butcher fixed his gaze on the floor. A tear made its way down his cheek.

"My father and my wife's father made our marriage. I am not a native of Chelm. Every day I struggle to understand this place and make my way here. I have done very well in the day to day business of the world, but I still fail to understand the wisdom of the Khakhomim of Chelm."

"So the Great Rabbi addressed a great evil when he removed this woman and this poor schlemiel from the congregation?"

"So it is said, and so it is celebrated. But I am only a butcher, and I find this beyond my understanding. Something about a string and the decency of the community…"

The rabbi from Berdicheva understood at once.

"Quite curious. Certainly not what I might have thought! So there was no terrible behavior that offended the community?"

"No. Some busybody must have made a fuss. Just a string that made a shed part of a house and made two people who really were never under the same roof sinners, offensive to G-d's decree."

"Thank you. Now, I must rest. Talmud study can be as exhausting as physical labor. I must restore my strength."

As he snuffed out his candle that night, the rabbi from Berdicheva said his usual prayers, and then begged HaShem to guide him, to show him how to bring some goodness and kindness into the lives of those who had been judged so harshly by the Great Rabbi and the Khakhomim of Chelm.

THE WONDROUS PLANS AND THE AMAZING FEATS OF THE CHIEF RABBI OF CHELM

Meanwhile, the Great Rabbi of Chelm paced the floor of his home, no matter how earnestly his devoted wife urged him to come to bed. How could he demonstrate to the Rabbi of Berdicheva, he wondered, how could he demonstrate to the entire world, for that matter, that of all men he was closest to G-d, peerless in piety, and unsurpassed in wisdom and judgment?

He stared out of his window, his mood low and bleak. The night was clear and the soft silver glow of moonlight bathed the synagogue of city of Chelm in a soft, unworldly and almost magical light.

"But how can I enjoy the beauty of the moon when my heart is so troubled? What can I do? What can I do?" Finally, he made his way to bed.

But, after only an hour of fitful sleep, the Great Rabbi arose. He dressed in his robes. Heedless of the hour, he awakened three strong and loyal members of the Sanhedrin.

"Fellow Khakhomim of Chelm, I worry whether our visitor from Berdicheva fully appreciates our wisdom and our dedication to Torah and Talmud. HaShem has spoken to me, and HaShem has instructed me to demonstrate our righteousness to him in a way that the esteemed Rabbi of Berdicheva cannot possibly misunderstand or fail to acknowledge.

"Yesterday, within his hearing, I explained why the light of the moon is more important than the light of the sun. Tonight, we will capture the moon itself, and bring it before him to show the power of our prayer and our understanding of the ways of HaShem."

He ordered these three strong members of the Sanhedrin to place a fine oaken barrel on a small cart, and to fill it halfway full of water. Then, with great care, the men followed his instructions to move the barrel on the cart to a place where the reflection of the moon would play upon the surface of the water it contained. When the image of the moon appeared directly in the middle of the barrel, the Rabbi shouted, "Now!"

The men quickly placed a heavy lid on the barrel, chained it in place, and the Chief Rabbi, who was a man of substance, sat upon it as the others conveyed the cart to the synagogue.

"Fellow Khakhomim! Let no man's eyes wander from the top of this barrel. We cannot allow the moon to escape, or we will look like fools before the Rabbi of Berdicheva. Now I will go home and prepare for tomorrow. Keep watch! Never divert your eyes from that top of that barrel!"

THE NEFARIOUS NOCTURNAL SINS
OF FIEVEL BEN SCHMENDRICK

As the night wore on, poor Fievel, still in search of warm walls to lean against, drew near to the barrel and the three men who stared at it so intently.

"Good Khakhomim," Fievel ventured, "What are you doing here in the middle of the night? Is this a new form of worship or prayer in Chelm, unknown to me?"

"Begone, Fievel!" shouted one of the three. "You are not one of us. If you were, you would rejoice that the Great Rabbi has captured the moon in this very barrel, and tomorrow will display this demonstration of his power to that overrated visitor from Berdicheva! I would thrash you if I had not been ordered never to remove my eyes from the lid of this barrel!"

Not daring to look toward the sky, Fievel scurried off down some loathsome and filthy alley, to spend yet another night huddled cold and alone.

THE GREAT RABBI OF CHELM
DEMONSTRATES HIS WISDOM
AND PIETY TO ONE AND ALL

T he next day dawned bright and clear. After prayers, breakfast, and prayers, the rabbi from Berdicheva and his students joined the Great Rabbi of Chelm, his Sanhedrin, his students, and interested members of the congregation.

First, a number of relatively minor concerns were discussed in great detail. These were classic Talmudic contemplations, such as deliberating over how to enumerate the actual number of plagues visited upon the Egyptians as the Israelites fled from slavery to freedom, whether there were deeper and as yet unappreciated meanings to the fact that Moses and his generation had to die before the children of Israel were permitted to enter the Holy Land, and finally whether there had been any new insights into dream interpretation since the days of Joseph.

With these preliminary issues resolved, and resolved in a manner that he hoped history would well remember, the Chief Rabbi of Chelm felt that the right moment had arrived! Now he would to demonstrate to one and all that through his prayer, piety, and wisdom, he now possessed the moon, and could claim his place among the greatest rabbis and scholars of all time.

The Chief Rabbi of Chelm stood and raised his hands. He drew them far apart, and brought them together with a thunderous clap. The Khakhomim of Chelm looked back and forth at one another. Never had such a thing been done! No one could remember any rabbi making such a dramatic gesture! Again, the Chief Rabbi of Chelm drew his hands apart and clapped. The room fell silent.

And then, one final clap, louder than those that had gone before! A door opened, and the three members of the Sanhedrin who had assisted the Chief Rabbi the fateful night before this glorious morning brought a small, narrow cart into their meeting place. One member of the Sanhedrin pulled the cart. One member of the Sanhedrin pushed the cart. A third member of the Sanhedrin actually stood on the cart itself, steadying a barrel that rested upon on the cart with one hand, while his other hand pushed down on the wooden top closing the barrel, pressing as hard as the situation allowed.

"My distinguished colleague from Berdicheva! Outstanding students of the Rabbi of Berdicheva! Distinguished Khakhomim of Chelm! Righteous students and members of this congregation, and any guests among us!

"Today you will witness the power of piety, prayer, and study! You will see with your own eyes what intellect, knowledge, and spirit can accomplish under the guidance of HaShem.

"I, your rabbi, your teacher, your judge, and your friend, shall place before you the light of the moon! Yes! The moon! Yesterday I explained why the light of the moon is more meaningful than the light of the sun. Just look outside at this fine day! It is bright all over. On such days we have little need of the light of the sun.

"But, here, to show you what can be accomplished by the power of the spirit and the intellect, refined by years of study of the Torah and the Talmud, I bring you the light of the moon!"

Everyone gathered around as close as they could. The Chief Rabbi of Chelm gave a signal, and the barrel was opened. As the first several people filed by in reverence, they either made exclamations of delight or broke into tears.

"It is so beautiful!" proclaimed the delighted.

"I must have sinned, so that HaShem will not allow me to see the light of the moon that the Great Rabbi has brought to delight the righteous!" wept those who felt they had failed to behold such a wonder because they were unworthy.

Finally, a young boy on the verge of his bar mitzvah came up to the barrel. He turned to his father and asked, "Where should I look, Papa! I cannot see the light of the moon."

As the boy's father writhed in distress, the Chief Rabbi drew near. "Don't worry, young man! I will help you to see the light of the moon!"

But as much as the Great Rabbi looked, he saw nothing, not a single trace remained of his amazing accomplishment. He turned to the three men who had helped him capture the moon.

"Did any of you take your eyes away from that barrel for a single second?"

Two immediately said, "No, Great Rabbi!"

But the third was slow to answer. "I do not remember looking away for a single moment. But as we stood guard over the moon, a man approached us and I spoke to him to send him away. Could I have looked away for a second? I think not, but I cannot swear before Adonai that I did not fail you." He fell to the ground, weeping.

"And who was this man who appeared in the middle of the night?" The Chief Rabbi tried to control himself, but he clenched his fists and shook with rage in spite of himself. "Who was this man?"

"Great Rabbi! That man was the outcast Fievel ben Yaakov Moshe."

"That terrible sinner? Bring him before us! And bring that disgraceful woman as well! We shall prepare ourselves with prayer as we await them." He turned to the rabbi from Berdicheva. "I am sorry, distinguished Rabbi. Such a shanda for an honored guest to have to endure! But order must be restored!"

"My young students have never seen such a thing. I wish to take them aside and prepare them. Please excuse us for a moment. Come with me, my young friends."

THE RABBI FROM BERDICHEVA PREPARES TO DO A VERY SECRET MITZVAH

When the rabbi from Berdicheva was sure he was alone with his students, he spoke with a directness and determination they had never heard from the man they knew to be a master of tact and discretion.

"This situation requires methods beyond scholarship and pilpul. You will show the people of Chelm the greatest respect while knowing that they are fools, and that some among them are dangerous fools. You will not challenge anything I say, even if it contradicts or differs from everything I have ever said before.

"Yossi! My rheumatism has worsened in the course of our travels. I will need a cart and horse to complete our journey to Vilna."

"Yes, Rabbi."

"Arrange for this with a gentile of good character. And purchase two large barrels, and a mallet."

"Yaakov! Judah! If things go badly, I will ask the Great Rabbi to send you to pray with this widow, and with this Fievel. When you pray with them, here is what you must tell them…."

THE GREAT RABBI OF CHELM UNMASKS THE SINS AND VILLAINIES OF THE ACCURSED FIEVEL AND THE UNHOLY ACTS OF A WITCH POSING AS A POOR WIDOW

When the men from Berdicheva returned to the large study room to which the widow and Fievel would be brought, it was so crowded that it seemed that every Jewish man in Chelm was in attendance!

"Last night," the Chief Rabbi tried to control his escalating temper as he confronted the shaking Fievel, "Last night you were seen near the place where three members of the Sanhedrin were guarding the light of the moon."

"What? Do my ears deceive me?" cried Fievel, "How can you capture the light of the moon? Why I saw...."

"That will be sufficient! You pretend to doubt my power to capture the light of the moon because you want it for yourself!" The Great Rabbi turned aside and appeared to pray. Then he turned back to Fievel.

"Do you dare to mock me?"

"Of course not, Great Rabbi! But I am afraid some evil force is making it hard for me to hear clearly. I could not have heard what I thought I heard. Of course I could not have heard such impossible things! What I thought I heard was absurd!"

"And what did you think that you heard?"

"I am embarrassed to say, revered Rabbi."

"Please."

"But what fool would say such a thing? Certainly not the Great Rabbi of Chelm!"

"Speak!"

"I thought I heard you speak of capturing the moon, the light of the moon. Surely, no one would be so foolish as to think he could do such a thing! Perhaps HaShem! But no mere mortal!"

"Blasphemy!" came a scream from the Sanhedrin. "Blasphemy! The Great Rabbi of Chelm can do that and more!"

"But...." Fievel stopped. Had black gone white and white gone black? He felt faint, and stumbled to the floor.

"I can see it all now," cried the Great Rabbi of Chelm. "You came upon three men of the Sanhedrin guarding the moon, which I had taken down from the sky! And then... And then, you bewitched them and stole the moon for yourself."

"Bewitched? I am no woman!"

"Yes! You are right! You must have had the help of that woman with whom you consorted! She must be your accomplice!"

"That poor soul? Great Rabbi, she is simply a poor widow, slowly starving to death! How can you think this of her? She was kind enough to let me take shelter in her shed."

"Shed? Bed? You two lived in sin, bringing shame to our community!"

"Great Rabbi! I have never been inside her home."

"The understanding of the Khakhomim of Chelm differs from your own! And HaShem enlightens the deliberations of the Khakhomim of Chelm, ensuring their perfect reasoning and their sound foundation in the holy books of our people. Be silent! Say no more!"

The Chief Rabbi turned, distracted by the wails of the woman who was being more dragged than led into their presence.

"Silence!" ordered the Chief Rabbi. When the woman could not control herself he raised his voice, and finally shouted. But, to no avail. A member of the Sanhedrin approached the woman, and simply clapped his hands over her mouth, muffling her anguished cries.

The Chief Rabbi nodded, and proceeded.

"The facts before us are clear. Drawing upon my years of study and prayer, and guided by the wisdom of HaShem, I captured the moon, to demonstrate the power of our G-d, our holy books, and the strength that can be drawn from our good deeds and prayer. Only someone of consummate evil intent, determined to defy HaShem, the righteousness of this congregation, and the wisdom of the Khakhomim of Chelm, would undo this demonstration of piety and goodness!

"Fievel ben Yaakov Moshe! What have you done with the moon? Shameful thief! Where have you taken it?"

"Honored Rabbi," said Fievel, "I find this hard to believe! I don't know how a man, no matter how profound his knowledge and piety, could capture the moon. Perhaps someone of your wisdom can imagine such a thing. But all I know are my daily prayers and how to make and repair parasols. Such things are beyond my comprehension.

"Distinguished Rabbi and Khakhomim! I am too ignorant and stupid to even imagine how to do such a thing! Cannot the wise Khakhomim appreciate that what may be possible for men of such wisdom as theirs is beyond my comprehension?"

A rumbling of comments among the Khakhomim suggested that Fievel's profession of abysmal ignorance might actually constitute a reasonable defense. After all, if capturing the moon required the greatest efforts of the greatest of rabbis, how could this nebbish have carried it away, and hidden it so successfully?

But the wise Chief Rabbi had anticipated such a clever argument. "My dear fellow Khakhomim! Of course, you are wondering how this humble man could accomplish such a deed! And, of course, in the eyes of most men, even most men of great wisdom, such reasoning would be convincing. But if we examine the problem in sufficient depth, we find that this man, like the beast that attacked our community many years ago, could only accomplish such a deed if he were assisted by the evil impulses of the world, which must have taken up residence within him!"

Fievel's hand went to his heart! It was beating so fast that he felt it would burst. "Me? Evil?" That was all the poor man could say.

"Hear him! He has confessed!" shouted a member of the Sanhedrin. Many beards wagged assent.

"Learned Khakhomim! Let us not be hasty in our judgment! Now let us hear from this wretched woman."

But try as they might to force the poor widow to speak, all she could do was weep and scream in abject anguish and distress.

"Learned colleague, Great scholar from Berdicheva – What opinion have you formed of these evil souls?"

The rabbi from Berdicheva nodded, appearing lost in thought as he stroked his beard. After what seemed an uncomfortably protracted silence, during which the tension in the room built, like the clouds gathering before a terrible storm, he cleared his throat and began to speak in a clear but quiet voice.

"Esteemed Chief Rabbi, Distinguished Khakhomim of Chelm, members of this distinguished synagogue, and citizens of this worthy town! For many years I have studied our Torah, and debated the meaning of the passages in our Talmud. I have sat in the cheders of sages and scholars in many great seats of learning. There are few matters I have not studied in depth and at great length.

"But in all my studies and travels, I have never encountered anything as remarkable as the circumstances that confront us here today in Chelm! They are truly beyond my understanding. Never have I heard of a dybbuk or any evil spirit inhabiting a fish. I remember well the noble efforts of dolphins to protect all forms of life in the waters when our people passed through the Red Sea, which Moses parted with the help of HaShem. To this very day, we honor those dolphins of blessed memory that lost their lives so bravely protecting others. I remember as well the great fish that swallowed Jonah and spat him up upon the shore.

"But the matters before us today are unknown to me. I sit among you, learning with you wise Khakhomim and trying to grasp new and surprising things. The only wisdom I have to share is to say, without misrepresenting my knowledge, is that I do not understand, and I am not qualified to advise you. Today, I sit among you as a student. You all know that when I am uncertain, I always try to err on the side of mercy, and try not to think ill of my fellow man."

"Well said," joined the Chief Rabbi. "Fievel and the widow deserve understanding and mercy. But Fievel and the widow are no more. They have been transformed into creatures that are no longer children of Israel! They have become the hiding places of the evil force. The spark of the divine that once inhabited their frames has already departed, and returned to the throne of HaShem. Please do not think for a moment, my revered colleague, that I would deal so harshly with my fellow man."

"That puts my mind at peace," said the Rabbi from Berdicheva. "But tell me, Great Rabbi and wise Khakhomim, if the evil force that has inhabited Fievel has taken the moon, how shall we recover one of G-d's most magnificent creations? Where are we to search? What are we to do?"

"Hmm!" mused the Great Rabbi of Chelm, "You instruct me well. Perhaps there remain enough of the persons these creatures once were so that they may yet be helped to turn once more to the good. Perhaps I have been too hasty. Let me honor your wisdom. Let us confine them until tomorrow morning, and convene yet again before pronouncing judgment."

"Great Rabbi," spoke the rabbi from Berdicheva, "Perhaps now I have a suggestion to offer."

"Excellent!"

"Great Rabbi! Behold Fievel, quaking in terror. Behold the widow too terrified to speak. Everyone here, from the Wisest Khakhomim to the simplest child, wishes for these two, who once were as we are still fortunate enough to be, only the best and kindest in life. It would be natural to assign the oldest and wisest among us to sit with them, and instruct them once again in the ways of righteousness.

"But in our zeal to purge evil from our midst, we probably have terrified whatever human elements remain within them, while the evil force afflicting them remains defiant. Perhaps we of years and wisdom will be too terrifying to them, and may make them too afraid to hear the sweet truths of the Torah.

"May I suggest that my two youngest students be asked to spend some time with them, instructing them. Their efforts must be private and uninterrupted. Is there a woman among this community who does not speak our language? I certainly would not want one of my students to be alone with the widow, and I certainly would want the privacy of their conversations to be complete."

"A thoughtful plan!" said the Chief Rabbi. "But upon whom could we call for such a duty?"

"Great Rabbi!" A voice came from the congregation. "Great Rabbi, perhaps I can be of some assistance to you and the worthy Khakhomim?"

The speaker, Moshe ben Benjamin, was a merchant newly returned from the East. A trader in spices and precious cloth, he often was away for long periods of time as he traveled with other merchants in great caravans across the vast expanses of Asia.

"Great Rabbi! As you know, my dear wife passed away just before I left on my last journey to the East. As I sojourned among many strange and different people, I was introduced to many men in many nations. Near Tashkent, I found a community of fellow Jews, who had wandered to that place years ago to avoid those who would have destroyed them. They were most kind and hospitable. They do not speak our language, though they are of our people, so scattered around the world after that shanda, the destruction of our Temple in Jerusalem. I grew fond of a daughter of that community, and spoke to her father. He told me to talk to him again when I passed that way on my return. He became convinced my love was sincere and he blessed our union. Well, I love my wife and I can speak to her, but she still knows almost nothing of the language we speak in Chelm."

THE RABBI FROM BERDICHEVA
MAKES FURTHER PREPARATIONS
TO PERFORM A MITZVAH

As arrangements were being made, the rabbi from Berdicheva spoke to his students once again.

"Yossi, bring the cart and what has been prepared to this place on the morrow. Yaakov, you will speak to this Fievel, and Judah, you will speak to the widow. Pray with them. But after an hour of prayer, catch their gaze, look into their eyes, and tell them these very words:

"'You will never be safe in Chelm. The Rabbi of Berdicheva knows that the evil impulse is not in you and is not in some creature residing in you or possessing you or directing you. It is not in either one of you, and certainly not in some unfortunate fish, however repulsive. But there is some evil thing happening here, and those who have already ruined your reputations surely will destroy you. On the morrow, it is likely that truth will be thrown aside, and that the Chief Rabbi will condemn you to some terrible fate. Do not think of going to some other town nearby. Every rabbi within miles venerates the Chief Rabbi of Chelm, and will already be speaking ill of you, and praising him for overthrowing your evil. Even if tomorrow a different decision is reached, there is no undoing the evil that is spread by ignorant or hateful tongues confident in their own wisdom.

"'If you wish to live, and find peace among a community of your fellow Jews, you must be prepared to follow everything the Rabbi of Berdicheva says, and everything we say on his behalf. If you do otherwise, you will die among those who will never say the Kaddish for you, will never light the Yahrtzeit candles for you, and will spit upon your unmarked graves.'

"Then, resume prayer as if nothing unusual had been said."

Judah started to ask a question, but Yossi silenced him with a gesture and a smile. Yaakov muttered, "HaShem, give me the courage. Give your strength to my stumbling words."

"Amen," said Judah.

"Amen and Amen," said Yossi.

THE KHAKHOMIM SEARCH FOR
THE STOLEN MOON

That night, as Yossi helped the gentile craftsman complete the final tasks involved in finishing the rabbi's cart, and as Judah and Yaakov prayed with a fervor they had never felt before, the rabbi from Berdicheva walked with the men of the Sanhedrin as they searched for the moon. Scouring every possible hiding place in the Jewish quarter of Chelm, they finally arrived at the river. From time to time, the rabbi from Berdicheva stole a furtive glance at the cloudy sky. Those who saw him do so chastised him in the dark.

"Why would you look up there in the sky? We know Fievel stole it and hid it, evil sinner that he is!"

"Ah, so right you are!" said the rabbi from Berdicheva. "How silly of me to rely on old habits and thoughts while so much that is new has been learned and so improves our understanding!"

Two men held a third man securely while he leaned over and looked under a dock. While he searched, the clouds must have parted. He saw a beautiful reflection on the water.

"The moon! The moon! I have found the moon!"

So eager was he to recover the moon so basely stolen from the Great Rabbi that he dove into the water to grasp it, only to fail. Another member of the Sanhedrin, upon seeing the reflection of the moon so marred by the ripples and waves created by the first man's efforts, reproached his comrade,

"You fool! You clumsy fool! You've broken it!"

The rabbi from Berdicheva said nothing. But the members of the Sanhedrin were profoundly distressed.

"What will we tell the Chief Rabbi? What will he think of us?"

Then one looked at the water once more and cried out, "Look! It has been healed. It is whole once again."

Yet another member of the Sanhedrin jumped in to retrieve the moon. His efforts failed as well, and the moon seemed shattered once again. There was worry and lamentation until, after several minutes, it appeared that the moon had become whole once more.

"Try a net this time!" said one. Still another man reached for the moon with the net, missed it, and fell into the water, as had those before him. Suddenly, they heard an enormous splash, as if a great Leviathan had leapt up through the water of the river, and crashed down into its depths once again. The man in the water screamed and begged them to hurry to help him get out of the water before some great beast consumed him. But as the others reached for him to pull him to safety, he looked up toward them, and then beyond them. He cried,

"Look! The moon! Someone put the moon back in the sky!"

So shocked were the rest that they lost their grips, and the man they were pulling to safety plunged once again into the river. When they finally retrieved their terrified comrade, they were uncertain what to do.

But now every last one of the Khakhomim was afraid of the water and whatever horrid creatures dwelt in its depths. Panic swept over them. One man voiced their worst fears, "Some evil force has come to this place! What unspeakable things might befall us if we remain here?"

He took one step back, away from the water, and then another and another. Without a word being said, the men turned and ran away, as fast as they could. They rushed to the home of the Great Rabbi. The rabbi from Berdicheva watched them run off. Instead of following them to the residence of the Great Rabbi of Chelm, he enjoyed the beauty of the moonlight as he walked slowly back to the home of the kind-spirited butcher.

There he offered up his usual prayers, to which he added some special prayers for the morrow, asking Adonai to watch over Fievel and the widow. Then he went to bed, and slept peacefully.

FIEVEL AND THE WIDOW FACE THE JUDGMENT AND WRATH OF THE KHAKHOMIM OF CHELM

After morning prayers, and after breakfast, once again the Jewish community of Chelm assembled. After the proper prayers and observances, they prepared to judge Fievel and the widow.

At the request of the Chief Rabbi, the members of the Sanhedrin who had searched for the moon the night before offered their accounts once again to all in attendance, exactly as they had reported them to him, the Great Rabbi, the night before.

One said, "We found the moon, Great Rabbi! But we lacked your special powers, and it was able to flee from our grasp."

"We had just captured it in our net when all at once it was gone! Our friend was pulled into the water. We heard an enormous splash, and suddenly the moon was back in the sky where not even the tallest of us could reach it, not even with that great big net on the longest pole," said another.

Fievel was summoned before the Khakhomim of Chelm yet again. The Chief Rabbi confronted him, his voice booming loud, confident, and certain.

"We found your hiding place! You hid the moon under the dock down by the river."

"What?"

"And then the moon took on a life of its own, and ran away from the men of the Sanhedrin."

"What?"

"And then, suddenly, there was a great splash and the moon was back in the sky."

"What?"

"So we know, Fievel, that you stole the moon and hid it away. Since no one saw you return to the barrel from which you stole it, it is clear that you had one or more accomplices from the world of witches, evil forces, and spirits."

Poor Fievel had not yet learned to hold his tongue in the presence of the great ones.

"What are you saying? This doesn't happen among the Jews! That idea is trafe, just like a catfish!"

"Exactly!" pounced the Great Rabbi. "You have abandoned the world of the Jews and looked for accomplices in the world of the goyim! You brought goyisha evil upon the Jews of Chelm! Shame!"

The Chief Rabbi paused. "And when these good men found the moon you had stolen, you not only invoked those evil spirits from a world that is not our own, but you called upon that terrible beast from which I liberated this community so many years ago! You have unleashed untold evil upon us!"

"But Great Rabbi! I was your prisoner all this time! How could I have done such a thing?"

"In the world of the goyim, evil women change form and fly through the night! While we thought the widow was under guard, her evil spirit from the world of the goyim soared through the air to protect your stolen treasure, and when it seemed she might fail, she called upon that great beast that took the moon into its jaws, leapt up to the heavens, and spat it back among the clouds before it plunged back into the watery depths!

"The efforts of all that prayer! All that sacrifice! All those years of study! All those efforts to do the best for the Jewish people, destroyed by Fievel, this widow, and that demonic fish, all in the grasp of the evil intent!"

The Chief Rabbi held up his hands for silence, and seemed to spend several minutes in prayer.

"HaShem's will shall be done. Whatever was Fievel, whatever was the widow, whatever was a fish – all have been transformed into the very essence of evil, and all must leave this world."

A cry arose from the Khakhomim of Chelm:

"Death! Death to those who would undo the work of goodness!"

The Chief Rabbi of Chelm turned to his visitor from Berdicheva.

"What do you think, my honored guest? What would be done in Berdicheva?"

"I am very glad you asked, because what we do in Berdicheva may be helpful to this righteous congregation and the scholarly Khakhomim of Chelm.

"Your judgment is just! But when we must take such terrible and drastic measures, our rabbis in olden days taught, and we still believe today, that when we must drive such evil out from our midst, we must drive it far, far away. It is an old belief, and some say it dates from before the days of the Temple. But it is our tradition, our way, and we honor it.

"As I look around me, and I do appreciate the overflowing loving kindness of the Great Rabbi, the Honored Khakhomim, and all the good people of Chelm, I do understand that the widow you will now condemn was born and raised among you, and that many of you knew and liked Fievel before his disgrace became known.

"I humbly suggest that instead of filling the two new barrels I ordered made with the good wine of Chelm to bring to my brother,

HaShem would look more kindly upon us all if we were to seal Fievel in one barrel, and the widow in another. I will change my route to journey along the rivers, hoping to draw that terrible creature away from Chelm. And then, some place far away from Chelm, and far away from where any people of any race reside, we will breach the barrels, and sink them in the deepest water. Perhaps in this way, we can at last execute righteous justice and remove this terrible threat to the good people of Chelm."

"The wisdom of Moses and all the sages of all generations speak through you, dear friend of Chelm," said the Great Rabbi. "If you will accept this burden, you, your wisdom, and your courage will always be remembered kindly among us!"

And so it was decided! A festive dinner was held to celebrate this resolution. Everything wrong was due to Fievel, the widow, and the terrible beast of the water, and soon all would be far from Chelm. There would never be any need to question the wisdom of the Chief Rabbi and the Khakhomim of Chelm. They would continue to be regarded as the paragons of wisdom throughout the world of the Jews residing in this wonderfully enlightened portion of HaShem's creation!

YOSSI TAKES HIS FIRST STEP TOWARD BECOMING A TEACHER OF THE TALMUD

When the rabbi from Berdicheva and his students returned to their lodgings in Mottel's home, Judah and Yaakov were confused and distressed.

"Rabbi," asked Judah, "I don't know what to think. The Great Rabbi of Chelm and the Khakhomim of Chelm have said hurtful words and accused Fievel, the widow, and some large fish of doing all sorts of evil things, and even of doing some things that seem impossible. Yet you teach us to look for evidence. Perhaps I am too young to understand, but I saw no evidence at all. You teach us not to judge so harshly as they judge people here in Chelm"

Yaakove broke in, "I am confused too, Rabbi. You have taught us that it is wrong to allow harsh and untrue words to do harm. Yet you agreed with the Great Rabbi and the wise Khakhomim when they said awful things. Can you explain this to us?"

The rabbi from Berdicheva smiled at his students. Then he turned to Yossi.

"Yossi! In not too many more years, you will be Reb Yossi. Prepare yourself by explaining to young Judah and Yaakov what our Talmud teaches."

Yossi's face turned red. He had never explained Talmudic law or ethics to anyone before that very moment. He thought of trying to find the right words to excuse himself from his rabbi's request, but he knew all too well that behind this particular warm and loving smile from the Rabbi of Berdicheva there was an invitation to take a new but frightening step toward becoming a mensch. A mensch stands up for what is right. Only a mensch should become a rabbi! Could he, Yossi, find what was right in this awful situation?

Yossi thought, "The Rabbi of Berdicheva trusts me to answer Judah and Yaakov! But do I trust myself? My bar mitzvah made me a man by Jewish law, but I prepared for my bar mitzvah for such a long time, and had so much help! Now, suddenly, without a moment to consider…."

"Yossi?" There would be no time to consider.

"Very well, Rabbi. I suppose no man is ever completely prepared to explain the Talmud, but every man, in his own humble way, must try.

"We are taught to be careful, to guard our tongues. We are taught that the hand of man can destroy what is nearby, but that the tongue of man can do harm, and even kill, everywhere its message is spread. Nasty gossip is sinful, and the one who gossips is looked upon with scorn. In most situations, we are discouraged from saying anything that even if true, could cause trouble or give someone a bad name.

"To stir up trouble by suggesting some thing is not right, to put forth words that are hurtful and not at all true, these are terrible acts.

"We have seen that in Chelm, tongues are not guarded, people rush to say things that cause trouble, and people speak what serves their purposes, even if what they say is not proven or untrue, and very hurtful. The hurtful talk and silly thinking that we have heard about this poor Fievel and the unfortunate widow are condemned by our laws, our sages, and our traditions.

"And we will not even speak of what horrible things have been said about the catfish! While we witnessed what befell Fievel and the Widow, we cannot speak of the catfish with any wisdom. We know nothing about that creature, or even if such a creature plays any role in this sad matter.

"The Talmud teaches us to speak gently in correcting others, and so many wise rabbis tell us how hard that is to do so without inflicting pain.

"So, Rabbi, it seems to me that you offered a gentle reproof in telling stories of your own limited ability to grasp things as the Khakhomim understood them. But when you found you could not move them, you continued to follow the Talmud in saying nothing to cause them distress or difficulty, or bring turmoil to their community. In choosing to do this, you not only followed the wisdom of our people, but you also, sadly, had to make an unwelcome choice."

"A choice?" asked the rabbi from Berdicheva.

Yossi turned red again. "Yes, a choice. If you openly advocated for the poor man and the widow, those Khakhomim would have remained convinced of their own very special wisdom. We would not have helped Fievel or the Widow, and we all might be thrown out of Chelm, with horrible rumors about our own terrible deeds rushing before us more rapidly than we could travel.

"So you followed the good impulse in a different way. You could not undo the harm already done to Fievel and the Widow by unkind hearts and evil tongues. Their lives in Chelm are over. So you propose to spread a cloak of caring over them, and yet leave behind no painful dissention among the Khakhomim of Chelm, who seem quite satisfied to continue as they are."

"Well said, my young scholar," said the rabbi with a solemn expression. But then this wise and wizened student of the Talmud and the Torah could not hold back a mischievous smile. He turned to Yossi and asked,

"But what do our holy books say about the plight of the catfish?"

Now it was Yossi's turn to be solemn. "A man's study of our holy books requires a lifetime, and even then must remain sadly incomplete. I will have to study more carefully before I respond to this much more challenging question."

"Shall these words of Reb Yossi be written in our great books?" smirked Judah.

"Not until he has looked into our holy books deeply enough to understand the circumstances of the catfish!" said Yaakov.

The Rabbi of Berdicheva poured a small amount of wine for his students, and said a prayer over the fruit of the vine. They sat and talked and laughed until it was time for the last prayers of the day, and for rest.

THE CONDEMNED ARE CARTED
OFF TO THEIR DOOM

The cart that the Rabbi of Berdicheva had ordered was well built and sturdy, and the horse purchased to pull it was strong and steady. The rabbi and his students took turns chanting prayers and discussing pilpul. They were never silent, lest the groans of Fievel or the widow draw attention of anyone they encountered to the contents of the barrels they carried. In fact, they chose a route that avoided the largest communities of Jews in that region.

Yet wherever they stopped and joined others in prayer, the tales of how Fievel and an evil woman stole the moon from the Chief Rabbi of Chelm were already on everyone's lips. Even when they had journeyed two days travel from Chelm, the Jews whom they encountered acted as if they were sure these people, this degenerate Fievel and this wicked widow, had done something wrong. But to steal the moon? Surely that was a metaphor! Just a poetic statement of a mundane misdeed! The Rabbi of Berdicheva purchased some used clothing from a merchant he met at morning services in a small synagogue in a small town along the way.

After a terrible week for the two condemned prisoners, confined as they were during the daylight hours in the two barrels, the rabbi from Berdicheva felt it would be safe to allow Fievel and the widow to sit on the cart with him in their new apparel, while his young students grumbled good-naturedly about walking as they progressed toward Vilna.

THE OFFICIAL EXECUTIONS OF
FIEVEL AND THE WIDOW

A few days later, long before daybreak, the rabbi from Berdicheva sent Yossi ahead with the widow and with Fievel. He told them to await the others, secure in a place of hiding, miles beyond a certain place deemed suitable for their executions.

When the rabbi from Berdicheva, Yaakov, and Judah reached that place, where the river ran fast, wide and deep, the rabbi and his young students prayed for several hours. They filled the two barrels part way full with small stones and earth. They cracked several staves of each barrel with the mallet. The barrels were pushed into the strong current, and sank out of sight within minutes. They said Kaddish for the name of the widow, and for the name of Fievel. Then the rabbi tore his own garments as a sign of mourning.

Thereafter, the widow would be the widow of a cousin of the rabbi's who had, in fact, died young, and Fievel would become the rabbi's youngest cousin and the widow's brother-in-law, eager to make sure his widowed sister-in-law reached her destination in safety. Fievel now walked along with the young scholars, who enjoyed his company, as he enjoyed theirs.

THE RABBI FROM BERDICHEVA PREPARES HIS FAMILY TO MEET THEIR LONG-LOST RELATIVES, AND YOSSI'S HEART IS STOLEN BY A FORCE MORE POWERFUL THAN THE GREAT RABBI OF CHELM

As they drew near to Vilna, the Rabbi of Berdicheva suddenly decided to break their journey, and take a day of rest from their travels. But before dawn he sent Yossi ahead with their horse and cart, to carry a message to his brother. Yossi wanted to ride the horse and travel more rapidly, but the rabbi from Berdicheva insisted that he take the cart instead. While Jews now could own and ride horses in most areas where they resided, it remained possible that matters remained more restrictive in Vilna or some village through which Yossi might travel, and he feared bringing trouble upon his young scholar.

When Yossi knocked on the door of the home of the rabbi's brother, it was answered by Rachel, the granddaughter of the rabbi's brother. Rachel immediately and forever drew the warmest of feelings from the young scholar and took complete possession of his heart. When the rabbi's brother finally came to the door, he saw two young people motionless, just gazing at one another. He quickly sent the girl away, received the message of the rabbi from Berdicheva, and made sure that Yossi received refreshment before he returned to where his party remained, resting for the day.

"Tell my brother that I understand, and my heart is heavy to learn of the death of our cousin. His widow will reside with us, and our youngest cousin, whom I have never met, must spend some time with us to meet his family, and bring us news of those so far away."

As Yossi retraced his journey, he found it difficult to concentrate on his prayers. His thoughts upset him. He was penniless student, an orphan with no family to call his own. Such a girl as this young beauty from Vilna, such a girl would never enter the life of a young, shy, and unaccomplished man of no means except as a vision of loveliness to be remembered, with heartfelt affection and wistful sadness, for the rest of his life.

THE RABBI FROM BERDICHEVA
AND HIS VILNA FAMILY REJOICE
IN THEIR REUNION

On a beautiful spring day, the rabbi from Berdicheva, his cousin's bereaved widow, his youngest cousin (who was the brother-in-law of his older cousin's widow), and his three students arrived at the home of the rabbi's brother's in Vilna.

While the rabbi from Berdicheva told the whole truth to his brother, he was wary of the reach of the Chief Rabbi of Chelm, whose fame and prestige was great indeed. The brothers agreed to keep these matters to themselves.

"There is always something new in the world to understand, even for a scholar like you, my brother," the rabbi's brother remarked.

"Perhaps. Perhaps. But perhaps while mankind no longer worships idols of stone, wood, or clay, or even of gold, we have foolishly deceived ourselves, and have come to worship idols of flesh and blood that are even more useless than those smashed by Abraham and Moses in days past."

"How shall we destroy the idols, the golden calves, of today?"

"I do not know. I pray to HaShem every day to enlighten me, but some days, it seems more people turn to foolishness than toward the path toward truth, and become so dedicated…. Yes, my brother – idolatry lives on, in the worship of those unworthy of respect, and of ideas unworthy of credence, and of laws unworthy of obedience.

"But it is good to sit with my brother, the kindest of all friends. Perhaps HaShem has just answered my questions. Love, respect, caring, and dignity. Could it be as simple as that?"

THE RABBI FROM BERDICHEVA
THINKS LOVINGLY OF YOUTH
AND HAPPINESS

The rabbi from Berdicheva was a thoughtful and observant man. Once, he too had been young.

After he had listened to what his brother had to tell him, he sought out the wisest rabbi in Vilna, and asked him a question. He was pleased with the answer. He asked his brother's oldest son a question. He was pleased with this answer as well. He smiled to himself, and said no more.

THE POOR WIDOW'S FORTUNES
BEGIN TO CHANGE

The widow had arrived in Vilna as thin as the reeds that grow by the side of the river. Slowly, she was fed more food. At first she was given little more than she had eaten during the worst months of her poverty. The rabbi from Berdicheva wanted to be far more generous, but the doctor who had been called to attend the widow assured him that such openhearted kindness actually might do the widow harm.

"Rabbi, too often when people are freed from prisons where they were given little more than bread and water, they do not live long to enjoy their new freedom. When they are released, they are given a feast and a surfeit of good food. Most often, they rapidly dwindle and die shortly thereafter. We do not know why. But we see this and have learned that slow and gentle steps are kinder to the human frame."

Provided with evidence he could not question, the rabbi from Berdicheva explained the doctor's advice to the widow, who was more than grateful for the modestly improved diet she was being given already. In several weeks, she was strong enough to offer to help wherever she was needed. She began to watch the children of Abraham, a middle-aged merchant whose young wife had died several months before.

A LETTER FROM VILNA

A year and a few months after the Jewish community of Berdicheva had celebrated the return of their beloved rabbi, a letter was delivered to him. The Rabbi of Berdicheva brought it to his study. There, he opened it with care.

The rabbi's brother had written,

"Deprived of duress and the scorn of the Khakhomim of Chelm, our cousin's widow appeared to be a different woman, lovely, and full of energy and joy. In the fullness of time, Abraham, the merchant, who had first loved her for how well she looked after his children, came to look upon her with yet a warmer form of love. They wed, and were happy together. Of course, everyone knew that they would have no children of their own.

"Everyone but HaShem. HaShem blessed them with a fine son just last week. And now everyone calls her 'Sarah.' I am sure I need not explain, dear brother.

"Your rascal Yossi is a respectable married man these days, bursting with happiness. Our Chief Rabbi of Vilna has declared that Yossi is a rabbi at last. He has been given charge of the youngest students in the cheder, and they love him and his funny and mischievous ways. Rachel grows larger and rosier every week, and the women of Vilna are undecided whether she is likely to deliver herself of a boy, a girl, or even twins.

"The ways of HaShem defy understanding by the minds of men. A month ago some men arrived with a large package for our rabbi. When he opened it, he found a magnificent new Torah, with a sky-blue cover laced with golden thread. The cover was embroidered, 'From a Grateful Jew in Honor of the Rabbi of Berdicheva.' From a note sent with it, I suspect your own congregation will soon receive a similar treasure.

"Why should such a thing occur? Because... Well, perhaps this may be part of the story.

"Remember poor Fievel --- Poor Fievel no longer! As he sought work in Vilna, a visiting English lord asked him to fix his parasol --- No! No! He called it an umbrella. Can you imagine? They now make a cloth that keeps the rain from those who use this amazing invention. Fievel repaired it, studied the cloth, made some still better umbrellas or whatever, and presented the lord with one of his own design in thanks for introducing him to the new innovation, this amazing cloth.

"Back in London, which is quite rainy, they say, the nobility and the affluent so loved Fievel's improved umbrella that the lord sent for him to come to that great city. Fievel remembered and followed your advice, and quickly took a name in the English style – Philip Newman. Yes, both appropriate and worth a tiny chuckle.

"Together they created a new business. My son visited him when he went to London. The lord's once shaky finances are improved and Fievel now makes umbrellas for the great and near great, and was awarded something that seems to mean he makes umbrellas for the king. I think my son said, 'By Appointment to His Majesty.' Who could have imagined such a thing? He sits at the eastern wall in the grandest synagogue in London, and he and his wife (Yes! His wife!) never tire of praising your kindness.

"There is a final bit of news, my brother. And I am not sure how you will receive this astonishing information.

"I remember that you had very strong feelings about Chelm, and preferred to break your homeward journey in Keszlow, which most do not esteem as a center of learning. I am sure you had good reasons for your choice.

"Not too long ago, in Chelm, the time for celebrating Rosh Chodesh, the beginning of the new month, was near. But the night was cloudy, and the members of the Sanhedrin sent to observe the first sign of the crescent of the moon to mark the new month could not agree that it truly had been seen. So, the Chief Rabbi of Chelm and the Sanhedrin made their way to the river, hoping to get a clearer unobstructed view of the sky, or to discern the reflection of the moon on the water.

"The Chief Rabbi decided that he could be sure whether he saw the moon if he could just lean out far enough over the fishermen's pier to get a clearer view. As you will recall, he is a man of significant proportions. As he leaned over, held steady by several members of the Sanhedrin, their strength failed them, and he fell over into the water.

"Everyone was shocked, of course. But as the Great Rabbi was being pulled toward shore, the water seemed to open up behind him, and he was sucked into the maw of an enormous fish. It flipped its tail as it dove for the depths, and he was never seen again! Your old friend, the butcher, was there. He described the beast as an enormous catfish, larger than any other catfish he had ever seen. But the Sanhedrin agreed that it could not have been a catfish, that instead the evil forces of the world, determined to defeat the Chief Rabbi of Chelm, the best of men, had sent yet another demon fish to Chelm to destroy him.

"Whatever the explanation, the ways of HaShem are mysterious indeed.

"They say that the new Chief Rabbi of Chelm was chosen because his beliefs were so much like those of the Great Rabbi before him. Should HaShem grant you as many years as Methuselah, and should you wish to journey to Vilna one more time, may I suggest, despite the fact that your wisdom far surpasses my own, that you that you chose a route that never takes you closer to the celebrated city of Chelm than three days of travel?

"I miss your company and wisdom, my brother. We may never lay eyes on one another in this life, but when I behold the new Torah in Vilna, and when you soon behold the new Torah in Berdicheva, I know HaShem will allow us to feel, for at least a moment, our brotherhood, our love for one another, and a touch of the honesty and goodness that is so very rare in this world."

SEVERAL SEASONS LATER, AND SEVERAL GENERATIONS LATER

One golden summer day several years thereafter, the Rabbi of Berdicheva was called to the throne of HaShem, and the flame of his soul returned from whence his divine spark had come. He had left behind a strongly worded document in which he urged his congregation to pass over more famous scholars, and to offer his teaching and scholarly rabbinic duties to the thoughtful Rabbi of Keszlow.

The Rabbi of Keszlow came to Berdicheva, and there he built a great center of Jewish learning. Students travelled from far and wide to learn from him and to experience his goodness as a person. A modest man, he is best remembered for the famous scholars he taught and encouraged, many among the greatest rabbis of their generation.

Yossi lived a long and happy life. His many sons all followed him in becoming great rabbis and scholars. One of his many sons' many sons became an early member of the movement that today is known as Hasidism. He traveled widely, and studied with the great rabbis of his day.

Ultimately, he was called to become a rabbi in Berdicheva. Indeed, Reb Levi Yitzhak became one of the most revered scholars and rabbis of his era, and is known to history by the name of the city in which he spent the most astonishing years of an astonishing career.

He is remembered as the Berdichever, or the Berdichever Reb. Eli Wiesel devoted a whole chapter to the Berdichever in his wonderful study of Hasidic Judaism, *Souls on Fire.*

When changing times required Jews to take names in the Christian fashion, the family name of some of Reb Levi Yitzhak's descendants became Rabiner, for indeed, his family had been, and long remained, a family of rabbis for generation after generation.

I am proud to be a descendant of the Berdichever Reb. That statement is not part of a folk story. It is part of my own history and heritage.

AN EPILOGUE

I took some notes on my unusual dream, and turned to other matters. I told my wife Estelle about the dream. "Enough about that article, and enough about Chelm," she said.

"I think I'll get ahold of Isaac Bashevis Singer's version of the Chelm stories," I told her. "Would you like to read them?"

"No."

That evening, I ordered some books on Jewish Folklore on Amazon.com. I would satisfy my own curiosity, but clearly, that last exchange probably would be the last discussion of Chelm and the Chelm stories under my roof.

Those were my thoughts as I drifted off to sleep. But I was wrong. Sometime in the middle of the night, I must have had a dream.

A smiling elderly man appeared before me. It just might have been my wife's late uncle Izzy, who had immigrated to the United States from Slonim, Poland, so many years ago. I was surprised to see that he looked like the first man in my first dream, the man who had begun to greet me in front of a synagogue.

Izzy was a sweet, gentle man, a student of the Talmud, a man whose epic Passover Seders were full of song and lasted forever. I liked him very much.

"Who could believe such a thing, Rishon? Had I not read it with my own eyes, had my great-grandson not downloaded it onto his own Mac, and printed it out so I could read it yet again and again, I would not believe such a thing could be! Shmutz! Shmutz, shmutz, schmutz!

"So… I see why you are…. I don't know what to call it.

"Let me see if I understand…. Some ah…. ah… Someone writes an article. It says something. Right? But to say this thing he says things about you and other people that are just not true, or says them in twisted ways that make black look white, and white look black. And the nasty things that are said! People can get hurt when such things are said…. Right, wrong, whatever! All these things are against the ways of the Talmud. Isn't it against the law to do such things? Ah! Who knows?

"So, Rishon, some Khakhomim read it and go crazy about it and publish it anyway. Oy! Such a thing is not good for those Khakhomim. It is not good for the people he says bad things about. And in the fullness of time, the man who wrote these things… He will not be happy about what he has done!

"And you told them these things! You said to them, 'Don't publish this shmutz! Let me write something for you about the need for dignity and respect in the way scholars talk about one another and about their work,' you said.

"So, Rishon, we live and we learn. We learn that in many parts of the world, scholars think it is important to be accurate. We learn that in some parts of the world, at least some scholars think it is important to write with respect for their subjects and for their colleagues in the field.

"But we also must remember that in Chelm things are different. And wherever it is more important to agree with some popular idea or some great person than to pursue the truth, whenever fear and ignorance create a new golden calf that some turn to worship, that place is Chelm.

"You know, Rishon, your words may never reach the ears of the Khakhomim of today, and if they do, they may not be heard as you spoke them.

"You know, Rishon, that I love the great books of all peoples and cultures. In the great plays of ancient Greece, we see that our shortcomings lead us, in our pride, to do wrongful things that bring upon us the wrath of the gods.

"Ah, Rishon! We do not live in the plays of ancient Greece! No great god or hero is likely to jump out of a box or climb out of a trapdoor and make things right.

"But it may be of some comfort to remember, Rishon, that in every land and time, for every one of the Khakhomim of Chelm who becomes puffed up and wanders down paths that stray from what is best, there may not be some heroic figure of Greek mythology making ready to leap onto the stage or to jump out of a trap door to make things right! But, for every such overstuffed person, there well may be a large catfish, whether a creature of nature or of metaphor, that lies in wait!

"Rishon, listen to your wife. When this all began, she nodded with sympathy and understanding. But, as things went on, do you remember what she said?

"That smart wife of your, my niece! I heard what she said. She looked at you with that look of hers. You know that look! And remember what she told you? She said, 'Those people! They can all go to Chelm!'

"Listen to her advice. You have said your piece. Leave these Khakhomim of Chelm for the catfish!"

A SECOND DEDICATION

When I found myself embroiled in the matter that ultimately prompted me to write *How Fievel Stole the Moon – A Tale for Sweet Children and Sour Scholars,* I appreciated from the first that my situation was difficult, and perhaps impossible. Once an offensive article is posted on the Internet, it is accessible forever, a loose cannon that will rumble about in perpetuity throughout the electronic universe. It cannot be taken back. It is there for one's colleagues, friends, family, and patients to encounter as long as there is an Internet or whatever technology may replace it as time goes on, regardless of the harm it may cause.

Therefore, the kindness and support of colleagues and others has been more helpful than I can find words to express. These individuals did not necessarily share my views about various issues in the mental health field. Among them were several whose opinions on certain matters are very different from my own.

While some knew my field in depth, and immediately recognized that the article in question was off base and that it contained historically inaccurate assertions and inaccurate allegations, others were simply appalled by the contemptuous and nasty nature of the remarks made within it. I will forever be grateful to all of them for their understanding and empathy.

Regardless of their gender, ethnicity, or religious orientation, they are the psychological descendants of the Rabbi of Berdicheva and his students, the Rabbi of Keszlow, and the Rabbi of Vilna. Much as the Rabbi of Berdicheva rejoiced to encounter the thoughtful and modest Rabbi of Keszlow and treasured his precious moments with his beloved brother, we can and we should celebrate our discovery of the presence of such good people in our lives.

I have expressed my gratitude to those who were kind and supportive along the way. As much as I would like to thank them here by name, the psychological descendants of the Khakhomim of Chelm are well represented among the scholars of today, and I would not want my remarks to cause these good people to be linked with me in any way that might be unhelpful to them.

Not a single person among those who offered me support, help, or guidance is likely to be swallowed by a large catfish, or the metaphoric equivalent thereof.

⇌ ⇋

I attribute my inspiration to tell a children's story to convey important "grown-up" values to the wonderful "Charley Brownstein" stories Rabbi Henry Cohen often included in his sermons at Beth David Reform Congregation in Gladwyne, Pennsylvania. Rabbi Cohen's clever takeoffs on the plights of Charles Schulz' classic *Peanuts* characters entranced the children of the congregation and hooked the children in the congregation's "grown-ups" as well. His loving approach to his fellow man contributes to the character of the Rabbi from Berdicheva, who, I came to realize as I wrote, reflects aspects of my grandfather Boris Rabiner, my wife's uncle Izzy Poll, and Rabbi Henry Cohen himself.

ADDITIONAL READING

For Readers interested in the subject matter of *How Fievel Stole the Moon – A Tale for Sweet Children and Sour Scholars,* I include some references.

Before I wrote my formal reply to the article that concerned me, I had seen it posted on line and I made the journal's editor aware of my concerns. I registered my objections to the article's inaccuracies. I stated that the reputations of several of those named in this article might be damaged by the erroneous and/or distorted or twisted statements that were going to be published about them. I suggested that in the place of publishing that article and my reply, in which I would have to make some rather strong statements in order to defend myself, I could submit a piece on dignity, decorum, and respect in scholarship.

Shortly thereafter, I was told that the article that concerned me would not be published. In preparation for writing the article I had proposed, I began to take notes and to assemble a bibliography. Two of the references I was collecting may be of interest to the readers of *How Fievel Stole the Moon.*

The first was Donna Hicks, Ph.D.'s wonderful book *Dignity: Its Essential Role in Resolving Conflict.* It was published in 2011 by Yale University Press (New Haven, CT). Dr. Hicks has been active in conflict resolution efforts in many difficult situations, and was a member of Archbishop Desmond Tutu's negotiation team in some of his peacemaking missions. She offers wonderful insights about the importance of respecting the dignity of others in efforts at problem-solving and conflict resolution. She makes a powerful and compelling case against approaching differences of opinion with a hostile or dismissive stance toward those with whom one disagrees.

I had also planned to cite Ronald Pies, M.D., who wrote *Becoming A Mensch: Timeless Talmudic Ethics for Everyone,* published in 2011 by Hamilton Books (Lanham, MD). His book is a short but thoughtful fascinating statement of Talmudic precepts, accompanied by contemporary vignettes that demonstrate the relevance of these precepts in situations we face in the twenty-first century. I freely admit that when I bought the book, I bought it for its title. But it proved to be a pleasant surprise, a deft and readable condensation of timeless wisdom. In the portions I had read, the text matched the title. After rereading *Fievel* a final time just prior to publication, I leafed through this book one more time and looked at the chapters I had not read before. I must recommend Chapter 13 in particular. It is entitled "Discussing and Criticizing Others Fairly." Although the words I attributed to Yossi came to me from my grandfather, I was pleasantly surprised to find that Chapter 13 (pp. 89-96) contains the very ideals that my grandfather and other Jewish educators had taught me almost 60 years ago. I added to the manuscript one precept mentioned by Dr. Pies that I had omitted in earlier drafts because I continue to question it. That will remain my personal struggle. Dr. Pies' work helped me to see that this omission did an injustice to the spirit of the argument that Yossi made in his explanation of Talmudic ethics, and belonged in the book.

I was dismayed when the journal reversed its decision, and decided to publish the problematic article, not withstanding its inaccuracies and nastiness. I was offered a chance to have my commentaries published as a response. With sadness and regret, I prepared my response for publication and put aside the project of writing an essay on the importance of dignity, decorum, and respect in scholarship.

While it is possible that I was exposed to some of the Chelm stories in my childhood, and no longer recall them, when Professor Davis began to describe them, I found them both fascinating and unfamiliar. I remember sitting in his lecture, and suddenly thinking that replying to foolishness by writing about the destructiveness that fools can bring upon the victims of their foolishness seemed like a more useful exercise than the scholarly response I had been drafting.

So, when I went home, I finished my scholarly response, and then immediately turned to writing the story of Fievel. The first draft of *How Fievel Stole the Moon* (my working title) flowed so rapidly that I could hardly type swiftly enough to keep up with my thoughts. Although I started *Fievel* in mid-afternoon, by the end of the evening I found myself, with feelings of both pleasure and astonishment, looking at both a reasonable outline and most of a first draft.

As I mentioned, to the best of my conscious knowledge, I had not read any version of the Chelm stories before I began to write. All I knew about them was drawn from the examples Professor Davis had used in his lecture. Nor had I ever read anything about shtetl life. My readings about Jewish matters had been primarily focused on issues related to the state of Israel and the aftermath of the Holocaust.

I simply threw myself into the project. I drew upon my empathy, my imagination, and my vague recollections of what I remembered from Hebrew School, and I wrote. I decided to just go with whatever welled up from inside of me.

Three weeks later, after completing the seventh draft, I paused briefly and began to read about the comedic tradition of Chelm, the city of fools. I was astonished to find that time after time I had come up with ideas and incidents similar to those that I found in the course of my reading.

However, my vision of the city of fools proved to be very different from the portrayal of Chelm in familiar folkloric accounts. Traditionally, Chelm is presented as a small town of Jews living in a rather rural setting and nearly isolated from the outside world. The citizens of Chelm are fools indeed. A collection of loveable bumblers, they are capable of turning any set of circumstances, however straightforward, into an absurd and comical web of misunderstandings and incompetence. Chelm's town meetings are exercises in the preposterous. Officials and civic leaders talk one another into one ridiculous thing after another. They reach remarkably astounding conclusions that all too often are self-defeating. In their relative isolation, they convince themselves that they are wise, but that foolish things somehow seem to happen to them. Others just do not grasp their wisdom!

So, the Chelm of my imagination proved to be a much darker domain than folkloric Chelm. In the Chelm of my imagination, the consequences of foolishness often lead to unsettling and disturbing outcomes. The Jews who reside in the Chelm of *Fievel* live in a section of the city that is pretty much their own. The Jews indeed have their own community, but they do interact with their non-Jewish neighbors. Instead of focusing upon the misadventures of town officials, town meetings, and persons who are considered wise, my story imagines the doings of the Rabbinic Courts of the era, Chelm-style, and wonders what misadventures might transpire within them.

The main historical inaccuracy in *Fievel* is that I unknowingly extended the power of Jewish authorities and tribunals over Jewish communities one or two decades beyond the dates on when their power was officially curtailed by the countries in which these Jewish populations resided. I had completed *Fievel* before I became aware of this discrepancy, and will claim, albeit retrospectively, the creative freedom accorded me under the terms of my recently renewed poetic license.

I am not an expert on shtetl life, and what little I thought I knew I am coming to believe was based on traditional stereotypes rather than firm grounding in fact. A very new publication, Yohanan Petrovsky-Shtern's *The Golden Age of the Shtetl: A New History of Jewish Life in East Europe*, published in 2014 by Princeton University Press (Princeton, NJ), challenges many of the stereotypes that long have been understood to be historically accurate. However, the period with which Petrovsky-Shtern's book is most concerned begins a century after the events of *How Fievel Stole the Moon*.

Earlier, I referred to the traditional spirit of the Chelm stories. I relish the deft ironic humor of those who retell them best. As I read their work, I often find myself either chuckling or laughing out loud.

Isaac Bashevis Singer's 1984 *Stories for Children*, published by Farrar, Straus, and Giroux (New York), is an enjoyable introduction to the gentler side of the wonderful, if topsy-turvy, world of Chelm. More difficult to obtain is his earlier portrayal of the Khakhomim, the wise men of Chelm, in *The Fools of Chelm and Their History*, a short book published in 1972, also from Farrar, Straus, and Giroux (New York).

Solomon Simon's *The Wise Men of Chelm & their Merry Tales* was first published in Yiddish in 1942, and in English in 1945. It was reissued in 1995 by Behrman House (Springfield, NJ). Solomon Simon's retelling of the Chelm stories is delightful and deliciously funny. Simon's gentle comedic touch and great timing enhance the stories, which are wonderful in and of themselves.

There are many other literary treatments of the foibles of the citizens of Chelm, but Isaac Bashevis Singer is a profoundly gifted author who won the 1978 Nobel Prize for Literature, and I really enjoyed Solomon Simon's work. The works of these authors are enjoyable resources with which to begin your acquaintance with what we might call the "classic" vision of Chelm.

Some readers may have been intrigued by the Rabbi of Berdicheva's challenge to Yossi, "But what do our holy books say about the plight of the catfish?" For those readers, I want you to know that the Talmud and the Torah are strangely silent on such matters. However, a secular answer might be found in extreme angler Jeremy Wade's 2011 book, *River Monsters: True Stories of the Ones Who Didn't Get Away,* from Da Capo Press (Cambridge, MA). But it might be more fun to track down the episodes of his television show, *River Monsters,* and enjoy the stories in which the wels catfish plays a prominent role.

Finally, I must mention Eli Wiesel's 1982 *Souls on Fire: Portraits and Legends of Hassidic Masters,* published by Simon & Schuster (New York). Wiesel's book is much more a wonderful study of the Hassidic spirit in Judaism than an overall scholarly history of Hassidism. Fievel's story takes place just before the rise of Hassidism. While Wiesel's book has little to do with *Fievel*, it has much to do with *Fievel*'s author. From my earliest years, my grandfather, a fully trained rabbi who turned from religion to science, taught me to be proud of our distinguished ancestor, Reb Levi Yitzhak, The Berdichever.

Why, you might ask, do I not provide a citation for the article that motivated me to write this book, or for my response to it? Here is my answer: When I said that the offending article should not have been published, and that I should not have been placed in a situation in which I had to either leave such reputation-trashing nonsense unchallenged, or write a critical rejoinder, I meant it!

Many thanks to my two expert readers, who went over earlier drafts.

I am grateful to Master Simon Drew Rosen, Certified Sweet Eight-Year Old, for his pithy and unflinching critiques.

I am grateful as well to Renee Parker, M.D., FACOG, FACS, LHRM, student of Judaica, Board Certified Obstetrician and Gynecologist, and Certified Mohelet (Practitioner of Ritual Circumcision), for her assistance both with certain terminology and with certain painful but necessary cuts.

And finally -- my gratitude and heartfelt thanks to Mila Perry, who created the wonderful and whimsical cover art for *Fievel*. She gave me exactly what I wanted.